THE AMARNA PRINCESSES : BOOK 1

OUTCAST

KYLIE QUILLINAN

First published in Australia in 2022.

ABN 34 112 708 734

kyliequillinan.com

A catalogue record for this book is available from the National Library of Australia

Ebook ISBN: 9781922852038

Paperback ISBN: 9781922852069

Large print ISBN: 9781922852076

Hardcover ISBN: 9781922852083

This is a work of fiction. Any similarity between the characters and situations within its pages and places or persons, living or dead, is unintentional and coincidental.

Cover art by Deranged Doctor Design.

Edited by MS Novak.

Proudly independent. Please support indie authors by legally purchasing their work.

This work uses Australian spelling and grammar.

LP10092023

ONE

TEY

I burst into the house, meaning to tell Papa about how I had just seen a man bite the head off a scorpion, and all without being stung, which seemed almost magical to me. Papa and my brother Intef, who was younger than me by two years, were sitting together on a rug. I retrieved my daggers from their various sheaths attached to my limbs and lay them neatly on a shelf.

"Close the door, Tey dear," Papa said to me. "I am sure the neighbours do not want to see how many weapons you have on your body."

"Better they know, so they do not think to be creeping around in the night," I said.

Papa was never comfortable with people knowing about my weapons, though, so I closed the door as he asked. I sniffed the air, hoping someone might have made dinner, but the only aromas were a bunch of marjoram hanging from a hook to dry, Papa's cypress and myrrh perfume, and the neighbour's jasmine shrub, the scent of which seemed to linger in the air even after I closed the door.

"What are you talking about?" I asked. "Intef has a funny look on his face."

"Nothing that concerns you," Intef said. "Why don't you make us a meal and let the men finish their conversation?"

Irritation filled me and I breathed deeply to calm myself, just as Papa had taught me. I set my fingertips against the smooth iron blade of one of my daggers. Its presence reassured me, even if I didn't intend to stab Intef with it. Not yet, anyway. Once I was sure I could speak without trying to kill him, I raised my eyebrows at him.

"Really?" I asked. "Do you want to re-think that?"

His expression told me he already regretted his words, but he would never admit it.

"No," he said, giving me an insolent look.

Before he could say anything else, I snatched a dagger from the sheath around my forearm and threw it in his direction. I had spent hundreds of hours practising this move but rarely had opportunity to use it. The dagger passed so close to Intef's head that it nicked his ear before it landed, tip first, in the wall.

"I thought you already put all your daggers on the shelf," Intef said as he touched his ear and looked at the blood on his fingers.

At least he had the sense not to scream or cry. He might annoy me, but he accepted his punishment without complaint. I could respect that.

"Stupid boy," I said. "As if I would leave myself unarmed. One never knows when a dagger will come in handy."

"Well, you have used it now," Intef said. "Maybe you could get around to making that meal?"

I grabbed the dagger from my other forearm sheath and sent it flying towards the wall. It nicked his other ear on its way.

"I think you can make your own meal," I said and went into the other chamber. My stomach growled, reminding me I hadn't eaten today, but I didn't want Intef to think he had won and I could hardly make a meal for myself but not Papa. My throat was dry and I wished I had at least brought a mug of beer with me.

I closed the door so they wouldn't realise I was trying to listen to their conversation. I already knew Intef was captain of the new queen's personal guards. The soldiers had been gossiping about how Pharaoh's senior advisors wanted their own man in the position, but the queen stood her ground. Intef had been only seven years old when he decided he was in love with her and he had spent the last eight years learning how to protect her with the aim of one day being her captain.

I would never have said it to him, but his single-minded determination impressed me. It motivated me when I wondered whether I should give up on my own goal of learning a soldier's skills. After all, it wasn't like I could ever work as a soldier. The idea of a woman soldier was ludicrous, but I had always felt drawn to that life. I could never explain why, even though Papa had asked more than once. It was my destiny, that was all I knew. My fate.

I couldn't make much sense of their conversation at first. They were planning a journey of some sort, although Intef wasn't the one who would be travelling. He had been charged with sending somebody — or more than one somebody — to a safe place. Once I understood that, it wasn't hard to figure out who they were talking about: the queen's younger sisters.

There were six princesses originally. The new queen was the third born. Two older sisters and one younger had all gone to the West. Her two remaining sisters were children, young enough to still grow their hair in the sidelock of youth. I had seen them as they rode in a palanquin on their way to bury their father who went to the West just a couple of weeks ago.

It seemed there had been some threat made against the youngest princesses. I guessed somebody — perhaps Pharaoh or his senior advisors — feared the young princesses being used by an opposing political faction to steal the throne. Intef feared the queen herself would be assassinated to make way for one sister or the other.

The queen had no desire for either herself or her sisters to be killed, so she ordered them sent away. That was Intef's task. He had to find a way for the two princesses to leave Akhetaten and escape to a place of safety.

My breath caught in my throat and for a moment, I couldn't think. I inhaled, held my breath, exhaled. I needed to be calm for this. I already knew I would volunteer to take the princesses. Not that I had any particular interest in the girls themselves — I had never wanted babes of my own — but the idea of fleeing the city with two princesses who were in danger of being assassinated gripped me. I had always believed I was meant for something *more* than the tedious reality of wife and mother. Something that would let me use my hard-won skills.

I would be their guard. Their guardian. I would keep them safe. We would travel to a new city. Maybe even a different country. We would know nobody and have nothing but each other. This was the destiny I had trained for.

When I opened the door between the chambers, Papa obviously knew what I intended even before I spoke. Perhaps he guessed from the look on my face, or perhaps he knew me too well. He didn't argue. I had made up my mind and he knew well enough that nobody had ever been able to dissuade me once I had. It was Intef who didn't understand.

"Fine," I said. "I will do it."

Intef gave me a blank look.

"Do what?" he asked.

"I will take them."

"Take what?"

I rolled my eyes. He wasn't as stupid as he pretended to be sometimes.

"Does your new queen know how dense you are?" I asked. "The princesses, obviously."

"Take them where?"

"I will figure that out. But for their safety, I will not tell you."

He shook his head, his face still bewildered.

"You are going to take my lady's sisters away?" he asked. "But who will guard them? Who will provide for them?"

"I will guard them. I will take them to a place where nobody knows who they are and I will keep them safe."

"But why? You don't even know them."

"Think of the adventure, Intef. We will leave and go somewhere new with nothing but our wits to keep us safe. This is what I have waited for all my life. This is what I have trained for."

"But what husband will want you with someone else's children trailing after you?"

"Have I ever said I wanted a husband?"

"But that is what—"

"Do not dare tell me all women want a husband. I do not. I will not be stuck inside, forced to clean up after a man and wash his clothes and bake his bread. I do not want to bear children and spend my life praying I will survive their birth and they will survive long enough to grow up. I want to be free. I want to live my own life. I want an adventure."

"But—"

Fortunately for Intef, Papa cut him off before he could say anything else stupid.

"I am very proud of you, Tey," he said. "But are you ready to walk away from your family and never see us again for the rest of your life? So long as they live, you can never return."

I went over to him and leaned down to kiss his cheek. When Papa was standing, he and I were of the same height, but sitting here on the rug right now, he looked much smaller than he was. It was the first time I had ever seen him look old.

"Dear Papa, I will be sorry to leave you and even sorrier that you will have nobody other than Intef to look after you in your old age. But this is what I have been preparing for. I am sure of it."

Papa rested his hand against the side of my face and gave me a sad smile.

"I know you do not ask for my permission," he said. "You have already decided and it is no less than I would expect of you, but go with my blessing, dear child. May Aten watch over you and your young charges."

"Thank you, Papa," I said. "Intef, I am going to get a couple of hours' sleep, but I will be at the palace at dawn. Bring them to the west entrance and make sure they are ready to leave. And take this."

I retrieved a dagger from beneath my shirt — it was the last one I had on my body, but he didn't need to know that — and held it out to him.

"I noticed you don't have one of your own," I said. "You will need one if you are to be the queen's captain."

Intef took the dagger from me. To my surprise, he looked like he was about to burst into tears.

"But this is your favourite," he said.

"And now it is yours."

I felt a little teary myself as I returned to the sleeping chamber to make my plans.

I supposed folk thought there was something wrong with me and I had often wondered if they were right. At seventeen, most girls my age were already married and had at least a babe or two, but ever since I could remember, I only wanted to be a foot soldier like my father. I admired the physicality of it. The discipline of training, the dedication to squad mates. The possibility of adventure and being in the heart of intrigue.

But of course a girl cannot take up her father's trade. If I wanted employment, I could have sewed or baked bread or brewed beer. I might have learnt to sculpt or carve or paint tiny beads for rich women to wear on the ends of their braids. Such crafts required talent, though, and I was lacking in any such thing except when it came to the skills of a soldier.

If I was a boy, they would have expected me to be a foot soldier. It was expected of Intef, although he too had chosen his own path. He didn't want to be merely a foot soldier, but the captain of the queen's personal squad. It had never before occurred to me to feel sorry for my father that he had two such independent minded children.

Having noticed my interest in his occupation when I was very young, Papa taught me how to use my dagger to take down a man, or to kill him if he was already down. He taught me other ways to kill a man too, ones that didn't need a dagger. I learnt to identify a trained man and one who carried hidden weapons, as well as how to tell when a man was trying to be unseen. I learnt to follow and be unseen myself, and I learnt to stay motionless for hours at a time. Sometimes I wondered whether my father was merely trying to keep me quiet and occupied when he bid me lie behind a bush or a large rock and remain out of sight for half a day.

When my father had taught me all he could, I used my ability to be unseen to spy on the soldiers as they trained. Not just my father's squad, but any soldiers I could find. I studied what they did, then practiced it myself. They ran laps of the city and hiked in the desert to make themselves stronger. They learnt how to survive on limited rations and even less sleep. I learnt those things, but even that wasn't enough for me. I spent countless hours tracking the wild creatures that lived outside the city of Akhetaten. Learnt how to feed myself with nothing but what I could gather or hunt. Learnt to find water in the desert.

As soon as I understood what the quiet conversation between Papa and Intef was about, I knew this was my life's purpose. This was what I had trained for. All those hours of instruction with my father, and many more hundreds of hours of training and practice on my own, it all led me to this.

The two princesses needed to escape and they needed someone to protect them. That someone would be me.

TWO
TEY

I spent the rest of the night lying on my bed mat, although I didn't let myself sleep. I didn't want to risk not waking in time, and besides, I had plans to make. I had to figure out where we could go. A place we would be safe, where nobody would think to search for us. But where?

I thought of and discarded various locations as I stared into the chamber's darkness. I had overheard enough of Papa and Intef's conversation to know the places they had already considered, and I ruled them all out. If Papa and Intef had thought of those places, others would, too. I couldn't risk going anywhere someone might think to look for us. So Greece, Hattusa, Phoenicia, the Mittani, and Nubia weren't viable options. Papa and Intef hadn't discussed Punt, so that was still a possibility. Or Rome, or perhaps even further afield: Indou or Babylonia.

But since they had intended to send the princesses away from Egypt, perhaps we should stay here instead. There were surely plenty of places we could hide away without leaving the country. We could go to the capital, Memphis. It was a big city and we would be just three more strangers in a place like that. But Pharaoh had previously ruled from Memphis — not the new Pharaoh, but the queen's father — and it was possible that at some point there might be a decision to abandon our desert city of Akhetaten and return the court to ancient Memphis.

Thebes perhaps. Another big city, just as ancient. But it was near the traditional burial grounds for our pharaohs and there might be reason for folk from Akhetaten — officials or some such — to go there. It would only take one person to recognise the princesses to shatter our safety. One person to see enough, or suspect enough, to lead pursuers to us.

Perhaps somewhere in the northern region, where the Great River made its way past a scattering of small villages and all the way to the Mediterranean. But outsiders would stand out in a village and it might be hard for me to find work. We needed some-where bigger. Somewhere we could be invisible.

I left my father's home for the last time an hour before dawn, even though I still hadn't figured out where I could take the princesses. Papa was still sitting on the rug where he and Intef had been speaking earlier. I should have known he would wait up for me. Intef was gone, presumably back to the palace to make arrangements for the princesses' departure. Papa got to his feet when I came out and gave me a long, searching look.

"I know what I am doing, Papa," I said. "Please try not to worry about me."

He enveloped me in his arms. I buried my face in his shoulder and tried not to let my tears fall. He didn't need to see me crying as I walked away. I inhaled the spicy scent of his perfume one last time and savoured the feel of his strong arms around me.

"I am so terribly proud of you, my dear," he said. "And I have no doubt you can keep them safe, but are you sure this is what you want?"

"I am certain, Papa. All my life I have felt like I was waiting for something, but I never knew what. This is it."

"You have never wanted to bear children. You have made that clear time and again. So why are you in such a hurry to take responsibility for these two girls? They are not like you. They will not have training or practical minds. They are princesses, probably spoiled and definitely pampered. They are exactly the kind of girl you despise."

"I have to do this. I cannot say why I am so certain, but there is something deep within me that says this is what I have spent my life preparing for."

"I cannot even hope to see you again, because if you were to return home, it would mean you had failed to keep them alive and I would not wish that on you."

"I am so sorry to leave you, Papa. I know a good daughter should look after her father in his old age."

"Don't worry about me, Tey dear. I can look after myself."

He squeezed me hard and despite my determination not to cry, I found myself wiping away a few tears that had somehow escaped from my eyes. I swallowed down a sob and my mouth tasted bitter.

"Do you know where you are going?" he asked. "Don't give me any details. Better that I don't know. If someone comes after you, they won't be able to force me to give up information I don't have. I only want to know you have a plan."

"I do, Papa."

I didn't feel bad about lying to him. If I told him I was leaving with no plan, he would spend the rest of his life worrying about me.

"I have thought of a place I can take them, which is so safe and so secluded, nobody will ever think to look for us there," I said.

He rested his hand against my cheek.

"I believe in you, Tey," he said. "I pray Aten will keep you and your young charges safe."

I hugged him one last time, then took my cloak from its hook. I slid my daggers into their usual places, in my waistband and the sheaths I wore around my arms and legs.

"Take this."

Papa removed the silver ring from his finger. He had worn it ever since my mother went to the West, along with my newborn sister. I had never seen him take it off.

"You know it was your mother's," he said. "I want you to have something of hers to carry. And maybe it will be useful one day. It is too plain to be valuable, but it might provide a few days' food or shelter if you have need."

As I took the ring from him, I noticed how his fingers trembled a little. He was trying hard not to let me see his pain. I slipped the ring onto my middle finger. It fit perfectly. A plain silver band engraved with the hieroglyphs for protection and peace. It still held the warmth of my father's skin.

"Thank you, Papa," I said. "I will never trade it, though. If we can ever return to Akhetaten, I will bring it back to you."

He nodded, and his eyes glistened with unshed tears.

"Go with Aten's blessing, my dear," he said.

I grabbed the end of a loaf of bread to eat as I walked. My stomach was growling fiercely and I didn't want to be distracted by my hunger. I knew as I walked away that I would never see my father again. Not in this life, anyway. As Papa had said, I could never return as long as the princesses still lived. If I was to be their sole protector, I could hardly leave them alone while I went to visit my family. And if they went to the West, I would have gone ahead of them. Nobody would get to them unless they had already cut me down.

As I made my way to the palace, the streets were mostly empty. I passed a fellow with two oxen and a wagon-load of something. The clopping of the oxen's hooves and the rumble of wheels were loud in the pre-dawn silence. Two dogs, three cats. Those were the only living creatures I saw.

I breathed deeply, trying to calm my mind and let go of my sorrow at farewelling my father so I could think clearly. I needed a plan before I took possession of the princesses.

All I knew was there were two of them and they were around seven and eight years old. Old enough to understand they were being sent away, but perhaps too young to understand why. I hoped someone at least tried to explain it to them before I took them.

At the palace, I found an unobtrusive place to wait. Far enough away so as not to arouse suspicion if the guards spotted me, but close enough that I could be at the west entrance within a minute or two. The door Intef was to bring the princesses to was visible from where I hid behind a row of young cypress trees.

I wasn't worried about the palace guards. I didn't think much of them. The best guards were assigned to Pharaoh's personal squad, although I took careful notice of the ones my brother selected for the queen's squad. They were all young men, some only just finished their initial training, but I could see why he had chosen each one. With time, he might shape them into a squad to rival that of Pharaoh's, but as yet, they were young and untried. The other guards, the ones assigned to watch the palace entrances and halls, were those with lesser skills. Still, I didn't need the distraction of fending them off while I waited for the princesses.

As the sun began to peek over the distant cliffs that surrounded the city, I slipped over to the west entrance. I had never spoken to the guard who stood there, but in the time I had watched him, I had already learnt he was unable to stay focused on his task. Even now, he leaned against the wall and busied himself with picking something out from under his fingernails. I snuck up behind him and hit him on the side of his neck. He probably never realised I was there before he lost consciousness.

I dragged him away out of sight. He would wake in a few minutes and be none the wiser as to what happened. I didn't want anyone to see me leaving with the princesses. I would leave no trail for anyone to follow.

Almost half the sun was visible above the cliffs before I heard footsteps from within the palace. Relief filled me. I had been starting to worry the guard would be up and wandering around before I could get away. I didn't want to have to kill him.

I stood to the side of the door, where I would initially be out of sight of whoever it was, in case it wasn't my brother. The door opened and Intef emerged with two young girls holding hands. The older one wore a gown of pale blue linen. It was too fancy for travelling in, but I supposed a princess might not own any plainer garments. At least she wore shoes and a shawl, and she carried a spare shawl, presumably for her sister.

It was the younger who worried me more. She was still in her nightgown and her feet were bare. Her face was red from crying and she sniffled loudly.

Intef looked relieved to see me.

"You are late," I said curtly.

I studied the princesses and for a moment, my courage failed. Could I really do this? Could I keep them safe? I couldn't let them see my doubts. They needed to trust me. So I swallowed down my fears and when I spoke, my tone was steely.

"Well," I said. "You look like a challenge. Come now, there is no time to waste."

I held out my hands to them. The elder grabbed hold. I gave the younger a stern look and she reluctantly reached for me. I held them tightly so they wouldn't get away if they struggled. At least the older one seemed compliant.

"Here, take these." Intef held out a small pouch. "I took a few gems from their mother's jewels. I suppose they would have received some when they got older anyway. They can wear them if they want, or maybe you can trade the gems for things they need."

I released the older princess while I took the pouch, although not without some reluctance. I wanted to rely only on myself, without the security of a bag of gems. Somehow that felt like cheating. But Intef was right that the princesses should have a share of their mother's jewels. Perhaps they would want something to remember her by, just as I had my mother's ring. I would hide the gems away until they were older.

"I am sorry I cannot requisition supplies or payment for you," he said. "The princesses must leave secretly and I don't want to leave a record that someone might notice and investigate. I hate that I cannot give you any reward, though."

I shook my head as I secured the pouch at my waist, then took the princess's hand again. Did Intef know so little of me that he thought I did this for payment or riches?

"Tey." His voice was lower this time. Maybe he didn't want the princesses to hear, although they could hardly help it, given they stood right beside me. "Are you sure about this? You are giving up your whole life. Even if you don't want to marry or bear children, surely there are other things you want. You won't be able to do them now."

"Look after our father," I said. "And do not try to find us. I will kill anyone who comes after us."

I didn't wait for his reply but walked away. The princesses scurried along, one on each side of me, their hands still firmly grasped in mine. The younger one's hand was sweaty, or perhaps she had been wiping the tears from her face.

"I don't want to go," she said.

She tried to stop walking. I had no intention of putting up with nonsense from a spoiled princess, so I ignored her and kept moving. The princess was almost swept off her feet and quickly decided it would be better to keep up with me than be dragged behind. That didn't stop her from complaining, though.

"I said I don't want to go." Her voice was louder this time.

Still I ignored her as I hurried them around the side of the palace. We needed to get out of sight as fast as possible.

"You have to listen to me," she screeched. "I demand you stop and listen."

She was making too much noise and would draw attention. I stopped and bent over so our eyes were at the same level.

"I am going to say this once and once only, so make sure you listen very carefully," I said. "My job is to take you away from here. However, I have not been told to keep you alive. If you make too much noise, if you give me too much trouble, I will cut your throat and be done with you."

She seemed to swallow down a sob. I felt bad about what I said, especially since she was already upset, but my priority right now needed to be getting them away quietly. I would do what I had to.

"Do you understand?" I asked.

She nodded, although her eyes brimmed with tears. She opened her mouth.

"No. Do not speak. Either of you." I shot the other princess a stern look, even though she hadn't made a sound. "We need to get away from here without anyone seeing us. You will not speak again until I give you leave to. Is that clear?"

"Yes," the younger princess whispered.

I glared at her and she realised her error. She nodded. When I looked at the older princess, she, too, nodded. Thank Aten she, at least, didn't seem like trouble.

"Let's go then," I said.

THREE
TEY

I f I was on my own, I would walk. I would follow the river and it would lead me out of the city. But I couldn't walk with two pampered princesses, one of whom wasn't even wearing shoes. We wouldn't get out of the city on foot. So we needed a boat. The palace sat right on the banks of the Great River and had two jetties which stretched out over the water. I found a place where we could watch the jetties without being seen.

"Stand here," I said to the princesses. "Be silent and don't move."

I couldn't barter for our transport, even if I had anything to trade. I wouldn't give up my mother's ring for such a thing and I wouldn't use the bag of gems. We needed to travel secretly, anyway. If anyone came asking questions, it wouldn't be long before someone remembered a woman negotiating transport, even if they didn't see the princesses. So I would have to steal a boat.

I knew little about boats, an oversight in my training which now seemed painfully obvious. All those hours I had spent running and sparring with my father, training myself to be still or to stay awake, to hunt, and to be unnoticed, but I had never thought to learn to sail. I doubted the princesses knew any more than I did, so it would have to be a small boat. Something I could manage by myself. A plan started to form in my mind.

"Come with me." I grabbed their hands and we hurried back around behind the palace.

To avoid the streets, I led them between houses and through people's gardens. The younger princess started to limp, although she didn't complain since I still hadn't said they could speak. She couldn't walk much further without shoes, though.

Down by the river, I found a stand of tall papyrus. I led the princesses over and pushed them into the centre. It grew densely here and would shield them from view. The papyrus rustled as we pushed our way through, but there was nobody nearby to wonder why.

"Wait here," I said. "I am going to get us a boat and I will come back for you as soon as I can. While I am gone, you must stay here and be quiet. Don't let anyone see you. Understand?"

They nodded, both looking like they would burst into tears at any moment. I supposed the gravity of their situation was sinking in. I didn't like to leave them alone, but I couldn't steal a boat and watch them at the same time.

"Here." I offered a dagger to the older princess. "Do you know how to use this?"

She gave me a wide-eyed stare and shook her head. At her age, I could already take down a man with my dagger, but I supposed it was too much to expect a princess might have learnt the same.

"Hold it like this." I pressed it into her palm and wrapped her fingers around it. "If anyone comes near, hold the dagger up and point it straight at them like this. Tell them that if they come any closer, you will stab them in the belly."

Her chin wobbled.

"I don't know," she whispered.

"Let me hear you say it. Come any closer and I will stab you in the belly."

She looked down at the dagger in her hand and shook her head.

"Say it," I said.

"Come any closer..." She choked on a sob.

"I don't believe you," I said. "Say it like you mean it."

"I don't think I can stab someone," she said.

"You don't have to stab them. You just have to make them think you will, and for that you need to sound like you believe it. Say it again."

"Come any closer and I will stab you." Her voice still wobbled.

"Make me believe you."

"Come any closer and I will stab you." She sounded more confident this time.

"I still don't believe you."

"Come any closer and I will stab you," she yelled, taking me by surprise.

"Much better. Stay hidden and look after your sister. Don't either of you go wandering. When I come back, I will whistle like this." I gave a long, low whistle. "Got it?"

She nodded and gripped the dagger more firmly.

I took off my cloak and sandals and set them tidily on the ground.

"Bring my things with you when I whistle," I said.

I hurried away, although not without a backward glance. I hated to leave them alone so soon, but I had to trust they had at least some understanding of the danger they were in. Surely they were afraid enough to stay hidden, for a while at least. I would have to hurry.

Back at the jetties, I found a place to hide and watch the boats. They were all too big, vessels that would need at least two people or even more to row. I kept still as I waited, not allowing myself to tap my foot or drum my fingers. At last, I spotted a suitable boat approaching, its sail billowing as a steady breeze pushed it against the current. It would be crowded with the three of us, but it was small enough that I thought I could manage it.

The man steered his boat into the wharf and lowered the sail. He secured the boat with a long rope, then retrieved a basket, which he swung in one hand as if it was empty. He must be fetching supplies of some sort. With no way of knowing what, or how far he had to go, I couldn't estimate how long he would be gone. I might not have much time.

As the man walked away, I hesitated. This boat might be his livelihood. He could be a fisherman, or perhaps he transported small quantities of goods up and down the river. Perhaps he and his family lived too far from Akhetaten to walk to the city when they needed supplies and relied on the boat for transport. I pushed away the thoughts. I couldn't afford to feel bad about stealing his boat. My task was to protect the princesses and I would do whatever I must.

I made my way downstream until I found a place where I could get into the water without too much difficulty. Cool mud squelched between my toes and the marshy scent of the Great River filled my nostrils, so pungent I could taste it. *Please Aten*, I prayed, *don't let there be any crocodiles or hippopotamuses here. If I get eaten, there will be nobody to protect the princesses.* Hopefully the busyness of the wharf would mean the larger creatures that inhabited the Great River spent little time in the near vicinity.

I submerged myself to my shoulders and waded back to the jetties. The little boat was still there and its owner was still gone. I needed to move fast. The water was much deeper here and I had to swim. I was careful not to splash or make any other noise which would draw attention and I tried not to think about what might be loitering beneath my feet.

When I reached the boat, I found hauling myself in more difficult than I expected. I had never done such a thing before and I underestimated how heavy my wet clothing would be. But I got myself in and lay on the bottom for a moment while I caught my breath.

I checked nobody was watching before I got to my feet and untied the rope securing the boat to the jetty. The oars lay neatly in the bottom. I had only rowed once before and for a moment I feared I wouldn't remember how to do it. But as soon as I felt the oars sliding through the water, it all came back to me.

I kept the boat close enough to the shore to stay out of the current, but not so close to risk being grounded. I listened for any sign I had been seen, but there were no shouts of alarm from the wharf behind me. Soon enough, I passed a bend in the river and was out of sight of the twin jetties.

FOUR
SETI

The woman shoved us into the papyrus and left. She moved so quietly that once I couldn't see her, I didn't know where she was. Nef and I stared at each other. Her face was white and her eyes big.

"I am scared," I whispered.

Nef screwed up her mouth as if she couldn't decide whether to reply or cry. I sniffled and a tear ran out of my eye. I wiped it away.

"What is happening?" I asked. "Why did Ankhesenpaaten send us with this mean woman?"

"I think she is taking us away," Nef said. "We are sisters to the queen now."

"But we haven't done anything bad. Does she hate us?"

Nef shrugged and fiddled with the edge of her shawl.

"I don't know," she said. "Maybe she thinks she has to send us away."

"But I don't want to go. Why do we have to?"

"I don't know, Seti. I don't know any more than you do. We will have to ask the mean woman when she comes back."

"If she comes back," I said. "Maybe she has been paid to take us somewhere and leave us there. The captain said someone might kill us."

"Well, if that was the case, she wouldn't leave us here, would she?" Nef said, rather sensibly I thought. "We could find our way back to the palace from here."

"We should go home," I said. "Before she comes back for us."

"I don't know. She told us to stay here. She left her sandals with us. And her dagger." Nef looked down at the dagger in her hand. "I hope nobody finds us. I couldn't stab someone."

"She said you didn't have to," I said. "It is all pretend. Don't come any closer or I will stab you in the belly. Remember?"

Nef gave me a grateful smile and offered me the dagger.

"Do you want to hold it for a while?" she asked.

"No. She said you had to."

Nef frowned. "Maybe I could put it on the ground until she comes back?"

"She is really quiet. What if she sneaks back and we don't hear her? She will probably yell at you if she sees you put the dagger down."

"I don't want her to yell at me," Nef said. "She is scary."

I edged a little closer to her. My arm caught on the spiky head of a baby papyrus, making it rustle.

"Shh," Nef said.

I had been trying to get close enough to hold her hand. It would have been comforting to have her fingers wrapped around mine. Instead, I stuck my thumb in my mouth. It tasted of salty sweat.

We waited for the mean woman to come back.

FIVE

TEY

It was harder than I expected to find the place where I left the princesses, but eventually I spotted the palm tree I had noted as next to where they hid. It was almost out of sight from my spot on the river, which I had not expected. I made a careful note of how different the riverbank looked from the water. I wouldn't make the same mistake twice.

I drew the boat as close to the shore as I could and whistled. There was no movement from the place where the princesses should be. My heart pounded. Had somebody found them? Had they run away? I shouldn't have left them alone so soon.

I whistled again as I looked for something to tie the boat to. But then the papyrus rustled and the older princess emerged. I had been looking in the wrong place. My position on the water had disoriented me more than I realised.

Relief crossed the princess's face when she saw me. She gestured for her sister to follow, and the two princesses made their way down to the water.

"Quickly." I held out my hand to the older one. "Throw me your things and get in."

She gave me a wide-eyed stare and I remembered I had said

they couldn't speak. We had both forgotten when we practiced with the dagger.

"Do you need to say something?" I asked.

"I cannot get in," she said. "It is all muddy here."

"This is as far as I can pull in the boat. You will have to go through the mud."

"But then we will need to wash our feet." She sounded like she was explaining something very obvious to me. "And we have no towel with which to dry ourselves."

I shot her an incredulous look.

"You are fleeing for your lives and yet you hesitate because you don't want to get your feet muddy?"

"I don't mind the mud," she said. "We just don't have a way to clean ourselves afterwards."

"Get in the boat. I don't have time for such nonsense. If I tell you to do something and the only way for you to do it is to get your feet dirty, that is what you do. Got it?"

Her chin wobbled and she wiped her eyes. For Aten's sake, was she going to stand there and bawl?

"Just get in." I tried to soften my voice. "Please. I am only trying to keep you safe, but we have to hurry."

Meanwhile, the younger princess was watching her sister, likely intending to follow her cue. If I could get the older one on board, the younger would follow. Especially if she thought I might depart with her sister, leaving her alone.

At length, the older girl moved. Mud squelched as she waded through, her skirt held high to keep it clean. When she reached the boat, she passed me her shawl, along with my cloak and sandals.

"Where is the dagger I gave you?" I asked.

"I wrapped it in your cloak when you whistled. I didn't think I would have to stab anyone if you were here."

She clambered into the boat and I gestured for the younger one to follow. She was quicker than her sister. Perhaps she was less worried about getting dirty. I would have to remember that. It might come in handy the next time we faced a situation like this.

As soon as both girls were on board, I used an oar to push us away from the bank. For a moment, we didn't move, and I feared the boat was stuck. But then it shifted and we slipped away.

"Get down," I said as I rowed towards the centre of the river. "I need you to stay out of sight until we are well away from the city."

I still hadn't decided whether to go north or south and I figured I would put the decision in Aten's hands. If the wind was strong, I would put up the sail and let it push us southwards against the current. If the wind was too weak, I would let the current take us north to the Delta.

The breeze was indeed strong, but it took me some time to set up the sail, having never done such a thing before. We drifted north while I struggled with it. Finally, the sail was up and it looked more or less correct from what little I knew. The sail caught the wind and we headed south. I heaved a sigh of relief once we were past the palace and its twin jetties. I had feared the boat's owner might have returned and was watching for his vessel.

The princesses huddled together in the bow, their faces white. The elder's eyes were red, as if she had been crying, and the younger had her thumb in her mouth, although surely she was too old for such a thing.

"Are we allowed to speak yet?" the elder asked in a very quiet voice.

"Yes," I said. "You can speak, but keep your voices down."

Establish something in common. Make this seem like a shared experience. That would help them trust me. Or at least that was what Papa said when he told me about how to build a rapport with a suspect. I had never had an opportunity to put that into practice, but I figured the same techniques would apply in this situation.

"This must be very scary for you," I said.

"Who are you?" the elder whispered. "Where are you taking us?"

"My name is Tey. I am Intef's sister. He is the guard who brought you to meet me."

She frowned. "He took us away from our sister and she let him. Why?"

"What did she tell you?"

"Nothing really," she said. "But Intef said someone wanted to kill us. Is that you? Are you taking us away to kill us?"

"Aten, no. I am supposed to protect you. I won't let anyone kill you. Either of you. Now, let's do proper introductions. Tell me your names."

"I am Neferneferuaten Tasherit." Her voice was proud, even though she huddled in the bottom of the boat. "I am the daughter of Pharaoh Akhenaten, may he live for millions of years. I am supposed to say that," she added as an aside, "because he went to the West not long ago. Everyone calls me Nef. My sister is Setenpenre."

"Seti," the younger princess said around her thumb.

"And you are sisters to the queen," I said. "Do you understand what that means?"

Nef shrugged.

"It means she is very busy and important," she said. "We only see her late at night now."

"I mean, do you understand what being the queen's sisters means for you?"

She looked at me blankly. Someone should have explained these things to them before we left. I hadn't expected to tell them myself. Aten damn you, Intef. I focused on the boat for a few moments, checking the sail and that we were still in the centre of the river. It gave me time to think.

"There can only be one queen, you understand?" I said. "But which woman is queen can change. There are people, very bad people, who might want a different queen. Someone who is not your sister."

"But she has to be queen," Nef said. "She is the oldest princess, so she must marry Pharaoh. That is how it works."

"And who would be the oldest if she went to the West?"

Nef seemed to swallow hard before she answered.

"Me," she said.

"So the bad people might kill your sister to make you queen. And because you are so young, they would control you. You would be their puppet and would have to do everything they said."

"But Pharaoh is more important than the queen. He was married to our sister Merytaten, but she went to the West. Now he is married to Ankhesenpaaten. He would stop the bad people from killing her."

"Pharaoh can still rule regardless of which sister he is married to, so long as she is the eldest," I said. "But the bad men might kill him, too, and force you to marry one of their own men to make him Pharaoh. Then they control everything."

"But Pharaoh is a living god," Nef said.

"That doesn't mean he cannot die like any other man." I wasn't sure how the living god thing worked myself, but their father had died and surely he was an ordinary man before he became Pharaoh. "But do you understand what I am saying? They would make you queen and force you to marry the man they want on the throne. Is that what you want?"

Nef shook her head.

"I don't want to be queen and I don't want the bad men to kill Ankhesenpaaten," she said.

"That is why I have to take you away. Your sister wants me to hide you so the bad men cannot find you."

"For how long?" she asked. "When will we be able to go home?"

I looked at her for a long moment, hoping she would figure it out. Hoping I wouldn't have to say it. Aten damn their sister for not telling them herself. But Nef just looked back at me and waited. They both did.

"You won't be going home," I said. "I am sorry. As long as your sister is queen, I have to keep you hidden."

Nef looked at me calmly and my heart sank as I realised she didn't understand. But as I searched for another way to explain, her chin wobbled. It seemed she had merely been digesting my words.

"Never?" she whispered. "Ever?"

"Never ever."

The princesses looked at each other, and Nef reached for Seti's hand.

"Did you hear her?" Nef asked.

Seti frowned at her. "We can never go home?"

Nef shook her head, and Seti's face crumpled. They leaned their heads together as they cried.

I focused my attention on the boat and the sail and keeping us right in the centre of the river. Let them mourn. The sooner they came to terms with the situation, the better. In the meantime, I needed to decide our next steps. So far, my entire plan comprised stealing a boat and getting us away from Akhetaten. Now I needed to figure out where we would go.

SIX

TEY

The princesses were quiet for some time as they came to terms with the news they could never go home. We sailed past several men standing knee deep in the water as they washed clothes. A couple of young boys splashed each other. Did their mothers know where they were? The river's banks were a dangerous place with the possibility of crocodile or hippopotamus. Surely that danger had been impressed on the boys. But they were not my responsibility. The two girls with me in the boat were.

At last we were far enough away that it should be safe for the princesses to sit up.

"You can get up now," I said. "Carefully though. Don't rock the boat too much or it might tip over."

They sat up and Nef rubbed her shoulder, holding her arm awkwardly.

"Are you injured?" I asked, sharply.

"Just stiff. I was lying on that arm."

I nodded and didn't know what else to say.

Nef straightened her gown. She folded the two shawls and laid them neatly in the bottom of the boat while avoiding looking at me.

"I am hungry," Seti said.

We needed food, and Seti needed clothes and shoes. Coming up with a plan could wait for now while I figured out how to get some basic supplies.

"We will get some food the next time we go past a village," I said. "Watch for houses so I can concentrate on the boat."

"Seti needs shoes," Nef said. "And she is still wearing her nightdress."

"I will sort that out as well."

It seemed Nef might have a streak of practicality, which was more than I expected.

The princesses lapsed into silence, and with nothing but the need to keep the boat steady to take my attention, I noticed my soaked clothes. Despite the warmth of the day, the cool breeze made me shiver. There was nothing I could do about my clothes, though. I could hardly take off my gown and sail naked down the Great River. The thought made me smile and I restrained myself. This was not a good time for the princesses to see me smiling. What I could do as we sailed was dry my daggers. I pulled them out of their sheaths and set them in my lap.

"Pass me my cloak," I said.

Nef handed it over without a word. I dried each dagger on the cloak and lay them in the boat. They would only get wet again if I returned them to their sheaths before my clothes dried. When I glanced up, the princesses were staring with wide eyes at my daggers. Perhaps they had never seen a woman carry weapons before.

They would have to pretend to be my daughters. That was the most logical reason for the three of us to travel together. At seventeen, I was a couple of years too young to be their mother, but I had often been told I looked older than I was — Papa said it was because I was too serious — and the princesses perhaps looked a little younger than they were since they still wore their hair in the sidelock of youth. Their sidelocks should have been shaved off two or three years ago, for Nef at least. So it should be believable enough, despite our ages.

But where were we travelling to and why did I have no

husband with me? Perhaps we had escaped him. He was cruel and I feared he would kill all three of us, so I took my daughters and ran. No, that might be a little too close to the truth, given we did indeed flee the possibility of murder.

Perhaps my husband had gone away for work and we travelled to meet him. He was a guard, or a craftsman. A skilled craftsman might be summoned to another village for a special commission by some wealthy patron. Or perhaps he had left us and we were searching for him.

No, he was dead. Killed in an accident. Or a drunken brawl. Or something else. I could figure out the details later. But for now, my husband was dead and my daughters and I travelled to family who I hoped might take us in. My husband's mother. She lived a long way away and had never met her granddaughters. I had no living family of my own, so I travelled to find my dead husband's mother.

It was a good story. Different enough that if anyone came asking questions about a woman who had stolen two princesses, nobody would think of the poor, bereaved woman whose husband had died, leaving her and her daughters destitute.

It was simple enough for the princesses to remember. All they needed to tell anyone was that I was their mother and their father was dead. It didn't matter if they couldn't remember where or to whom we travelled. Nobody would expect children of their age — children still coming to terms with the loss of their father — to understand the details. And if they became teary while telling their story, because it made them think about their father or how they were forced to leave their sister, all the better. It would make the story sound more genuine.

My husband's mother needed a name and a location. I decided to call her Henuttaneb. My father had a sister of that name. She went to the West several years ago, but her name would be easy for me to remember. I didn't want to risk my mind going blank when someone asked the name of my dead husband's mother.

We travelled south, so I needed a southern location. A village where anyone we encountered wouldn't be likely to know someone or to be from themselves. Nubet perhaps. It was the southernmost village I knew.

If we encountered someone from Nubet who said nobody by the name of Henuttaneb lived there, I would feign shock and devastation. This was where my dead husband had said his mother lived and I didn't know what I would do now. Nobody would press too hard for details past that.

The plan felt good. It wasn't too complicated, so I wouldn't be in danger of forgetting it or muddling the details. It should be easy enough for the princesses to remember, and the parts they were likely to forget weren't important anyway. Nef's voice interrupted my thoughts.

"I can see houses over that way." She pointed. "Do you think it is a village?"

"Well spotted," I said. "It likely is."

It took more effort than I expected to row us out of the current's grip and we had gone well past the village by the time I managed to get the boat over to the bank. I found a spot to pull in, then pointed towards the rope which was coiled in the boat's bottom. They may as well start learning how to be useful.

"Nef, take the rope and tie it around the trunk of that tree just up from the bank."

She looked down at her feet. The mud had dried by now, but she made no attempt to clean her feet while we sailed, despite her earlier distress about the possibility of dirty feet.

"Make sure the rope is good and tight, then you can wash your feet in the river. I will try to get something you can use as a towel while I am gone."

"You are leaving us?" she asked, very quietly.

I meant to leave them with the boat while I ran back to the village.

"Seti doesn't have any shoes," I said. "And it will be quicker if I go by myself. I can be there and back in half the time it would take if we all go."

"But what if the bad men find us?" Nef asked. "Do you think they know we are gone yet? Are they already looking for us?"

I had impressed on them the concept of the bad men so they would be more willing to do what I said. I hadn't anticipated it would make them afraid to be without me. It was obvious, really, but I had little experience with children other than my brother.

"We will have to walk back to the village," I said. "It might be a long way and there won't be any paths. Seti, can you manage that?"

Seti looked from me to her sister. Nef nodded encouragingly.

"I think so," Seti said. "But if my feet get sore, will you carry me?"

"No, I won't carry you. If you say you can walk, you will walk the whole way. It will be too bad if we get halfway there and your feet are sore. You cannot come back to the boat by yourself, so you will have to keep going. Are you sure you can do that?"

Seti frowned and jammed her thumb into her mouth. Wasn't she supposed to be only a year or so younger than Nef? The difference between them seemed much greater, but maybe this was normal for their ages.

"Seti? I need you to make a decision," I said.

"I can walk," she said from around her thumb.

"Well, then," I said. "Nef, get that rope tied so the boat will still be here when we get back and let's go. I am getting pretty hungry myself."

Nef clambered over the side of the boat, landing in the water with a splash. I handed over her sandals. Her skirt was already soaked, but she still held it up as she made her way over the muddy bank. She struggled to get the rope around the tree as her arms weren't really long enough. I waited in the boat and kept my mouth shut. No point offering to help her. It would only set an expectation that I would do the hard things for them. If these princesses were to survive, they needed to learn to look after themselves.

"I have done it," Nef called at last.

"Are you sure you tied it tightly?" I asked. "We cannot afford to lose the boat. If it floats away, we might have to walk for a long time before we find another boat. Days probably."

She tugged the rope and her forehead creased as she examined her knots.

"I think so."

"Good," I said. "Seti, out you go."

Seti looked like she would object, but Nef called her and she got up. She fell, rather than climbed, out of the boat, landing in the water face down. She got up, shook herself off like a dog, and clambered up the bank.

I followed her, pausing to check Nef's knots. They didn't look like any knot I knew, but they seemed sound enough.

"I think that will hold," I said.

Nef gave me a small smile and I held out her sandals to her.

"Come on," I said. "To the village."

SEVEN

TEY

My clothes had dried as we sailed, except for where I had been sitting on my gown. The village wasn't as far behind us as I thought. It was an easy walk for me, but the princesses quickly grew tired and lagged behind.

"Keep up," I said over my shoulder. "The sooner we get there, the sooner we can get something to eat."

They tried to walk faster, but soon dropped behind again. Maybe I should leave them somewhere? I could run on ahead, get what we needed, and be back within the hour. It wasn't all that far. But what if someone found them? What if they got scared and tried to make their way home? No, I had told them that once they started walking, they would have to go all the way. They needed to learn I meant what I said.

"Come on," I said. "You need to walk faster."

We waded through grasses which were only knee high to me but taller for the princesses. I prayed Seti wouldn't step on a cobra or viper with her bare feet and made sure to make plenty of noise as I pushed through the grasses. Nef's skirt caught on a branch when she passed too close to a bush. She snatched impatiently at the fabric and made a soft sound of annoyance when it tore.

They were puffing and red-faced long before the village came into sight. I would have to leave them somewhere now, though. I didn't want them to see what I was about to do.

"Right," I said. "I will go get food and some clothes for Seti. See the shady patch beneath that dom palm tree? Sit yourselves down there and do not move until I get back. Understand?"

"We aren't coming with you?" Nef asked. "You said we would go all the way to the village."

"And you did," I said. "But now I need you to wait here."

"Why can we not come with you?"

"It is better if nobody sees you yet. We are still too close to Akhetaten and the risk that someone might recognise you is too high. So wait here in the shade and I will be back as soon as I can."

"What if the bad men come while you are gone?" she asked. "Aren't you supposed to protect us?"

"Here." I offered her a dagger. "Just like last time. You remember what to say?"

"Don't come any closer or I will stab you in the belly."

Nef took the dagger from me and I didn't miss the way she squared her shoulders. Now she had gotten used to the idea, holding the dagger made her feel braver.

"When we stop for the night, I will start teaching you how to defend yourself," I said. "For now, if anyone sees you, just pretend you know what you're doing, but I will show you for real. All right?"

"All right." She looked happier now. "Come on, Seti. We are going to go sit in the shade."

She took Seti's hand and they went to the dom palm tree. I waited long enough to see them sit down, then I ran. The village was only a few minutes away, at least at the pace I could move alone.

It wasn't much. Less than two dozen cottages. I made a wide circle around it, examining each house, noting where the villagers were and which cottages appeared to have nobody at home. That one there had a vegetable garden which looked like it had a few things ready to harvest. And the cottage next door had clean laundry drying over a bush. There was a gown which might be only a little too big for Seti and a linen sheet I could use to carry the vegetables. If that gown belonged to a child, they might also have a small pair of sandals.

I waited until there was nobody around, then darted over to the first of the cottages I had chosen. The shutters were closed and the air inside smelled stale. Half a loaf of bread, hard and a couple of days old, but something in our bellies was better than nothing. A small piece of cheese. A handful of onions and a bowl of dates. I couldn't see a basket or a pack of any kind, but a length of linen hanging from a hook on the wall was probably the occupant's shawl. That would do, and the princesses could use it as a blanket at night. I dropped the food onto it, and tied it so I could carry it easily. A quick search of the other chamber didn't reveal any child-sized sandals.

I listened at the door to make sure nobody was approaching, then slipped back outside. I grabbed the child's gown and the linen sheet, then darted over to the garden next door. More onions, a lettuce, two fat cucumbers. I wrapped them in the sheet. It wasn't as much as I had hoped for, but we could make it last a couple of days if we needed to.

EIGHT
SETI

I stood close to Nef as we watched Tey walk away.

"I don't think she is supposed to leave us alone," Nef said.

I shrugged.

"I am hungry," I said. "If she doesn't bring back some good food, I am going to be really mad."

"Maybe she will bring a roasted hen."

"Ooh, and some goat stew," I said.

"And some melon juice."

"Roasted fish with lentils."

"Fresh bread," Nef said. "Where do you think she will take us to sleep tonight?"

"Maybe she knows a palace that is not very far away," I said.

"I need a bath. My feet are still dirty and the mud smells bad. She said I could wash them in the river, but I didn't get a chance."

"When we get to the palace, you can get a servant to wash your feet," I said. "They will bring a bowl of water, just like at home."

"I hope they put blossoms in the water," Nef said. "I like it when they do that. It makes my feet smell sweet."

"They can wash my feet, too." I looked down at my poor, dirty feet. "They hurt a lot."

"She said she would get you some sandals."

"But we still have to walk all the way back to the boat."

"Nuh uh," Nef said. "She couldn't expect us to walk so far again. I think she will bring a palanquin back with her."

"And slaves to carry it?" I asked hopefully.

"Of course, silly. It is not like she could carry it herself."

"Or maybe a sled, if she cannot find enough slaves. She could probably drag a sled with both of us in it."

"She does look very strong," Nef said.

"Did you see all her daggers?"

"Even Mother's guards never had that many daggers," Nef said. "And I have never seen a woman with a dagger."

"I don't think she is respectable."

I wasn't quite sure what this meant, but the servants talked about how some women were respectable and some weren't. They never explained, though, or at least not when I was listening.

"Here she comes." Nef gave a great sigh, as if she hadn't expected Tey to come back. "She has got food for us."

Tey carried two bundles. I figured one had food and the other must have sandals and clothes for me.

"No palanquin," I said, a little mournfully.

"And no slaves." Nef sounded almost angry. "She cannot expect us to walk back to the boat. Not after you walked all the way here without sandals."

Tey didn't smile or even wave at us as she approached.

"I wish she would smile more," Nef said. "She looks very scary when she doesn't smile."

"Maybe she is supposed to look scary," I said. "She is supposed to be our guard, after all."

"Who ever heard of a woman guard?"

Tey was close enough to hear us, so we stopped talking about her.

"Food?" I asked as she reached us.

"Enough for a couple of days," she said.

"I am starving." I sniffed the air as I reached for one of the bundles. I was almost certain I could smell roasted fish. My mouth watered as if it could taste the fish, too.

"You can eat when we get back to the boat," she said, snatching the bundle out of my reach. "Come on, the sooner we head back, the sooner we will get there."

"I am too hungry."

"Later." Tey's voice was stern. She started walking without even asking if we were ready to go. "Come on, then."

Nef and I looked at each other and neither of us moved. Tey stopped and turned back to us.

"I am hungry, too," Nef said. "And Seti gets cranky when she is hungry. I think it is best if we eat now."

"You can eat once we are out on the river and not a moment earlier." Tey glanced back towards the village, then gestured for us to follow her. "Hurry up."

"Did you get sandals for Seti?" Nef asked, still not moving.

"I couldn't get any. I will get some the next time we stop. She won't need shoes while we are on the boat anyway."

"Her feet are already sore," Nef pointed out. "She cannot walk all the way back without shoes."

"Well, I couldn't get shoes, so she will have to manage," Tey said. "There is something the two of you need to understand. Your pampered lives are over. I am here to protect you and keep you alive, not to fetch and carry for you. There will be no more palaces, no more servants, no more getting everything you want. I will protect you and I will teach you to look after yourselves, but I will not do everything for you."

I sniffled and a tear ran out of my eye again. Why was she so mean? Did she like making us cry? Maybe it made her happy. She was probably jealous she wasn't a princess herself.

"We have stayed here too long," Tey said. "I can hear someone following and it might be one of the bad men. Start walking."

Nef and I looked at each other again.

"Maybe we should go?" she whispered to me.

I shrugged. I was hungry and my feet were sore, but Tey was mean and I didn't think she would let us eat until we did what she said. When Nef started walking, I followed her.

NINE
TEY

I set a brisk pace and tried not to let them see I watched from the corner of my eye. Seti limped and even Nef seemed to be in pain, despite her sandals. I supposed they might never have walked so far before. Princesses had slaves to carry them in palanquins and save their delicate feet from injury.

"Stop," I said. "Seti, show me your feet. How bad are they?"

She raised her legs one at a time to let me inspect her soles. They were so dirty that it was hard to tell whether they were blistered or worse. A smear of dark brown along one heel might be blood or just mud. Making her walk barefoot in this condition was cruel. Yes, she needed toughening up, but not by being forced to walk on injured feet. At least, not yet.

I tore a few strips off one of the linen sheets and wrapped Seti's feet.

"There, that is the best I can do for now," I said. "Next time we go through a village, I will try to get some arnica for you to rub on your feet. This should at least be more comfortable in the meantime."

Seti scrubbed the tears from her cheeks. She took a couple of steps and nodded.

"Much better," she whispered, although from the look on her face, I wasn't sure she told the truth.

"What about you?" I asked Nef. "Why are you limping?"

She slipped off her sandals to show me the blisters where the straps had rubbed against her skin. I tore more strips of linen and wrapped her feet as well, still listening for any sounds of pursuit.

"Let's go," I said. "We should be able to move faster now."

"Would you like me to carry something for you?" Nef asked.

A peace offering perhaps. I didn't need help, but I also didn't want her to feel rejected.

"Thank you." I passed her the lightest of the bundles, the one that contained the vegetables I stole from the garden.

It seemed to take a lot longer to get back to the boat than it had to reach the village. I was getting pretty hungry myself by then, but I had trained myself to function effectively, even if I missed several meals in a row.

"I am so hungry," Seti said. She lagged behind again.

"We haven't had any breakfast today," Nef reminded me.

"You won't die of hunger for having missed a meal," I said.

"I am so hungry my hands are shaking," Seti said.

"The faster you walk, the sooner we will be back on the boat and eating," I said.

I stopped responding to their whines after that and eventually they fell silent. When we reached the boat, I let out a sigh of relief, then hoped the princesses didn't hear it. If the boat had been gone, we would be stuck here. If they couldn't walk what was probably not even half a league without blisters and complaints, they certainly wouldn't be able to make it to the next village. I tossed the bundles into the boat.

"Nef, go untie your knots," I said. "Seti, in you get."

"My bandages will get wet," Seti said.

"Take them off then and put them back on once you're in the boat. Best you wash your feet anyway."

She gave me a surly look, then sat down to untie her bandages. She moved painfully slowly and Nef had unraveled her knots well before Seti even had the first bandage off. My fingers itched to do the other one for her, just to hurry her up, but I restrained myself. She needed to learn to do things for herself. And they both needed a clear understanding that I was not their servant.

Finally, both princesses were in the boat. I pushed it away from the shore.

"Oars, Nef," I said.

She passed them to me and I rowed out to the middle of the river, where we caught the wind.

"Now can we eat?" Seti asked.

"Go ahead," I said. "We have to ration the food, though, so you cannot have much. Just enough to keep you going for now."

They eagerly unwrapped the bundles and pulled out the hard bread, the tiny piece of cheese, and the raw vegetables.

"Is that all?" Nef asked.

"It was a very small village," I said, rather shortly. "They didn't have much to spare."

And I had to steal even that much for you, you ungrateful brat.

"There isn't any hot food," Seti said.

I bristled at the whine in her voice.

"Of course there is nothing hot." I kept my gaze on the river, knowing my face probably revealed how incredulous I felt. "How did you expect we would make a hot meal on the boat?"

"I thought you would have brought it with you. From the village."

"It wouldn't be hot by now even if I did."

"You don't seem to have tried very hard to get food we will like," Nef observed.

I took a deep breath and tried to rein in my temper. If I had known how annoying they were, I might have thought twice about offering to take them away. Papa had said they would be the kind of girls I despised, but I didn't listen.

"Like I said, small village. If you are hungry enough, you will eat. I am afraid there won't be any..." What *did* princesses usually eat? "There won't be any roasted duck or melon juice on our travels."

"I don't like roasted duck very much," Seti said.

She reached for the bread and raised it to her mouth.

"No you don't." I leaned forward to snatch it from her. "That is for all of us to share and we need to make it last. Here." I broke the bread in half, then tore one half into three pieces. "We will share this half now and keep the other for tomorrow."

I handed them each a piece.

"Why is yours bigger than ours?" Nef asked.

"Because I am bigger than you. I need more food."

"But—"

I shot her a glare.

"I have had enough of listening to you two for a while. You can have this and this." I tossed a couple of vegetables onto their laps. "We need to save the rest. I don't know how far the next village is. I will hunt when we stop for the night and we can have a hot meal then, but for now, this will keep you alive. That is the purpose of food, after all. To keep your body functioning. It doesn't matter whether you like the food or if you enjoy the meal. You eat to nourish yourself. If you don't want to, that leaves more food for the others."

I bit into my bread and returned my attention to the river. There was no sign of boats either behind or ahead of us. It was just the three of us and the river birds and probably a few beasts somewhere down below. I tipped my face up to the sun, enjoying Aten's heat on my skin, the taste of bread on my tongue, and the cries of the birds that wheeled overhead.

Thank you for letting us get away safely, I prayed to Aten. *Thank you for letting me find food for them and transport. Thank you for letting me keep them safe this far.*

TEN

TEY

Despite their dissatisfaction with the meal, both princesses ate everything I gave them. They were silent for a while after that. Seti seemed barely able to keep her eyes open.

"You can go to sleep if you want," I said. "There should be just enough room for you to lie down if you take turns."

"Lie down, Seti," Nef said, moving over a little. "You can put your head in my lap."

Seti lay down. Was that the first time she had done something without complaining? I would like to think it was because I was making progress with her, but she was probably just tired from the walk.

While Seti slept, Nef seemed to alternate between looking down at her sister and watching the riverbank. This seemed like a good moment to try to build a rapport with her. If I could establish a relationship with one princess, surely the other would follow.

"Have you ever sailed before?" I asked.

"A few times," she said. "There was a festival for Aten once when my father took us out on a barge and we sailed along the Great River. I was pretty little, though. I don't remember much other than that there was so much gold on the boat, the sun shining off it hurt my eyes and gave me a headache."

"I have never sailed much before either, but my father taught my brother and me to fish. That is a skill that will be useful now."

I was tempted to add there wasn't any gold on the one boat I had sailed on, but swallowed down my snarky comment. That wouldn't help me build a rapport with her. I couldn't think of anything else to say, so I pretended I was busy with sailing and Nef went back to watching the riverbank. This area was full of tall grasses and papyrus. Herons waded through the shallow waters, their grey wings glistening in the sunlight. I thought I spotted the eyes of a hippopotamus watching them. I heard nothing but the wind and the splashing of the water and the birds.

Some time later, Seti woke and the princesses swapped places. Nef was a little taller than Seti and her feet touched mine as she tried to get comfortable. She pulled them back as if they burned. I moved a little to the side to give her more room. She shifted restlessly for a while but eventually seemed to fall asleep.

The sun had begun its descent towards the horizon by the time Nef woke. She spoke to Seti, a quiet question I couldn't hear. Seti shot me a look and shrugged. I looked away and tried not to feel hurt at being excluded. I had given up my home and my family to keep them safe and yet they whispered secrets between themselves.

It was time to look for a place to stop for the night. I manoeuvred the boat out of the current and let it drift along until I found a sheltered place to pull in. I nodded towards the rope in the bottom.

"Off you go then, Nef," I said. "Secure the boat."

She frowned at me.

"I did it last time."

"Yes, you already know how to do it. You did a good job with the knot last time, too. Kept the boat nice and secure. That is what we need again."

"Why cannot you do it?" she asked.

"Because I have done my share. I have done the hard work of sailing all day while you two slept. It is your turn to contribute now."

"Seti can do it."

"Seti will learn to do it another day. Today, you will do it."

"I don't want to."

"Fine." I set the oars back in the water. "We will keep sailing. If you won't secure the boat, we won't be stopping for the night."

"We cannot sail all night."

"You think so?"

"But we cannot sleep in the boat. There is not enough room for both of us to lie down. And you promised us a hot dinner."

"Everyone needs to contribute for things like that to happen. If you don't want to contribute, we don't stop for the night."

We had already caught the current by the time she changed her mind.

"I will do it," she said.

"Too late." My tone was curt.

A long pause.

"Tey, I am sorry."

"Apology accepted."

"Aren't you going to take us back to shore?"

"I already said we are not stopping now."

"But I told you I was sorry. I said I would tie the boat."

"It is too late. We have passed the spot I was going to stop."

"But you can find another, right?" she asked. "Or we can go back?"

"I told you if you didn't get out and secure the boat, we would be sailing through the night. You made your decision."

"But I changed my mind."

I shrugged and didn't look at her. In truth, I was pretty tired after no sleep last night and my stomach was so empty it hurt. I had planned to catch a duck and cook it over coals, but that would have to wait for tomorrow now.

"I need to pee," Seti said.

"Either hold it or go in the boat," I said.

"I cannot hold it," she said.

"We cannot go in the boat," Nef said. "That is disgusting."

I sighed.

"I think we are still misunderstanding each other," I said. "If I tell you to do something, you do it. If you don't, there will be consequences which will not be avoided just because you change your mind or say you are sorry. My job is to protect you. I don't care whether your feelings hurt or your bladder is full or you miss your hot meals. As long as you are alive, I have done my job. That is all I care about."

"You don't care if we are hungry or miserable," Nef said. "You don't care if we have to sit in a puddle of pee or we have sore backs from being in a boat all day."

"Nope."

"You are a monster," she said.

"And you are alive."

They ignored me after that and made a point of whispering between themselves. I kept my focus on the water and the wind and our surroundings. I had spotted a boat some distance behind us a couple of hours ago, but it was gone now, likely pulled into shore for the night. The stench of urine told me at least one girl had been unable to hold her bladder any longer. It would likely drip down between the planks soon enough.

But when I next looked down, a long trickle had made its way to our stolen supplies. I said nothing. I could make do without food for a while longer and it would reinforce the lesson I was trying to teach. I did move my cloak, though, before it got wet too.

As the moon rose and the air cooled, my tension eased. Here on the river, we were safe as long as we kept moving. Nobody would pursue us at night. No men, at least. The river beasts would gladly make a meal of us, but we were out of reach of them. The chirping of insects and water sloshing against the side of the boat filled my ears. I would be quite happy to do this forever. Just sail along the Great River through the night with no company but myself. It would be much more pleasant than trying to manage two spoilt princesses.

They seemed to be trying to stay awake all night, although now and then one of their heads nodded and they would awaken with a jerk. Were they trying to prove they could stay awake if I did? Or did they refuse to allow themselves the comfort of sleep in the hope I would coax them to lie down? Or something else I hadn't thought of?

If I could understand their motivations, I would be able to do a better job of establishing a rapport with them. I hadn't done very well so far. Papa would be ashamed of how I had let my emotions fuel my reactions. Tomorrow I would have to do better.

ELEVEN
TEY

As dawn broke, sending a riot of colour across the sky, I edged the boat out of the current and over to the shore. The princesses sat up a little straighter and rubbed their eyes.

"This is a brief bathroom break." Despite my resolve to do better, my voice was curt. "And you will clean out the boat."

Nef shot me an incredulous look.

"Surely that is your job," she said.

"I was not the one who peed in the boat," I said.

She looked down at the puddle of urine which had soaked through our supplies.

"The food," she said.

"And Seti's new gown. The food is probably ruined, but the gown can be washed."

Seti pursed her mouth. I thought she would say something, but she only looked away. Perhaps she, at least, was learning I wasn't interested in their whines.

I took the boat as close to the shore as I could and gave Nef a pointed look. Without comment, she took up the rope and climbed out. She splashed through the water and found a tree to secure the boat to, then looked at me, as if expecting praise. I ignored her and gestured for Seti to get out.

From the state of their clothes, both princesses had released their bladders. Fine, they could both share the work of cleaning up. I pulled the boat up a little further and tossed the bundles onto the bank. My own bladder felt like it was ready to burst and the constant stench of urine wasn't helping.

"You may as well deal with those first," I said. "Wash Seti's gown and see if any of the food is salvageable."

Nef glared at me, but I busied myself with ensuring the boat was as far up the bank as I could before I went behind a bush to empty my bladder. By the time I came back, Nef had untied the bundles.

"Oh, that stinks," she said.

I didn't respond.

"It is all over the food," she said. "We cannot eat any of this."

"I suppose it depends how hungry you are," I said. "I won't be hunting until we stop for the night, so if you want anything to eat before then, you will need to sort that out yourself."

Nef picked out the soggy remains of the bread and tossed it into the river, although not without a disgusted huff. She examined the vegetables.

"I suppose these might be edible if we wash them," she said, at last.

"Good," I said. "Why don't you start on that? Seti, you can wash the gown I got you. It will dry soon enough in this heat."

"We can stop long enough for it to dry?" Seti gave me a hopeful look.

I hadn't realised she was so eager to get out of the nightclothes she had worn since we left Akhetaten.

"Probably not, but even a wet gown will be better than staying in your nightclothes. May as well wash them too, so at least you will have something clean to change into when you need it."

Seti frowned at me.

"I cannot wear a wet gown," she said.

I shrugged. "Your choice. It is your nightclothes or the gown. There are no other options."

"I don't have a change of clothes," Nef said. "What about me? I wore this gown all day and all night and it smells bad."

I refrained from pointing out that the main reason it smelled was because she had wet herself. Instead, I pointed to the bundles.

"That is everything we have. If you want something else to wear, that is what you have to work with."

Nef studied her options.

"I could wear your cloak," she said at last.

"No, that is mine. I might need it."

She sighed and poked one of the linen sheets I had carried the stolen goods in.

"I suppose I could wash this and wrap it around myself while my clothes dry."

"Good idea." I hadn't been sure she would think of that. "I suggest you start with the clothes. Once they are clean, you can drape them over bushes so they dry while you deal with the boat. They might even be dry by the time you are done."

It would depend on how thoroughly they cleaned the boat. Given the distaste both had shown for the urine-soaked bundles, I suspected they might do a decent job.

Nef rinsed the vegetables in the river and set them on a rock to dry. Then she and Seti stripped off their clothes and washed everything else. They tried to drape them over bushes as I suggested, but weren't quite tall enough. I would have helped if they asked but they didn't, so their clothes were left halfway across the bushes with the hems trailing on the ground.

I searched the riverbank for anything edible and found some tubers and three duck eggs. My mouth watered at the prospect of a gently cooked duck egg. I could already taste it.

"Might as well clean the boat before you put on anything else," I said as Nef started to wrap one of the wet lengths of linen around herself. "It will give that a chance to dry anyway."

She shrugged and draped the linen over a bush. They were a couple of years past the age when children usually went naked, but neither seemed concerned. The princesses then tackled the boat. I might have expected they would have questions, but it seemed they were determined to ask me for nothing.

They consulted between themselves, then used their cupped hands to splash fresh water into the boat. They tried to tip the vessel up but didn't have the strength to do it. I looked away before they caught me watching. There was another whispered conversation and I felt them looking at me.

"Um, Tey," Nef said at last. "Would you be able to help us with the boat?"

"What do you need?" I tried to make my tone amiable. They would see that if they were civil to me, I would be civil back.

"We need to tip the boat up, but it is too heavy."

I went to the boat and tipped it on its side.

"Like this?" I asked.

"Hold it a little higher, please," Nef said. "So the, um, liquid runs out."

I raised the boat and once it was empty, the princesses splashed clean water in and scrubbed it as best they could with some pieces they tore off one of the linen sheets. At last, they were satisfied with their job and Nef instructed me to set the boat back down.

"If everything is clean, we should get moving," I said.

I wrapped the tubers and eggs in my cloak and set it on the floor.

Cleaning the boat took so long that their clothes were almost dry by now. Nef wrapped a piece of linen around herself and managed to tie it so it wouldn't fall off. She helped Seti into the stolen gown, then bundled up their other clothes, along with the vegetables she had saved. I waited until we were back in the middle of the river before I said they could eat.

Without a word, Nef unwrapped the bundle containing the vegetables. She started to pass a cucumber to Seti, then hesitated.

"What would you like?" she asked me.

"A cucumber, thanks."

She handed me one and passed the other to Seti before selecting something for herself. The cucumber was crisp and I couldn't hear anything over the sound of my own crunching. It still smelled faintly of urine and it tasted a little odd. I waited for one of the princesses to complain, but they said nothing. So, they were learning.

TWELVE
TEY

The princesses didn't speak much during the day, or not to me at least. As the afternoon warmed, my eyes drooped. I sat up straighter and made myself pay more careful attention to our surroundings. I had been awake for well over twenty-four hours. This was what I had trained for, though. I could manage two days without sleep and still function well enough. I could last a third day if I had to, although by then my thoughts would be confused, my reflexes slow, and sometimes I would see things that weren't really there.

Around midafternoon, I started watching for a place to stop for the night. I found one sooner than I expected and figured we could all do with the extra rest. Given the princesses were trying to be compliant, I wanted to reward their efforts.

"Are we stopping?" Nef asked as I began navigating the boat out of the current's grip.

It was the first thing either had said to me since Nef asked what I wanted to eat.

"This looks like a good place to pull the boat in," I said. "If we don't seize the opportunity, it might be a while before we come across another suitable spot."

When I drew the boat up to the bank, Nef reached for the rope.

"I think it is Seti's turn this time," I said.

Seti shook her head, but Nef spoke to her quietly. There was a brief, whispered argument between them before Seti grabbed the rope. She secured the boat and we unloaded our provisions. I checked Seti's knot and tightened it.

"We need to walk inland a little way," I said. "It isn't safe to sleep this close to the water. Seti, do you need to wrap your feet first?"

She looked down at her feet, considering.

"How far?" she asked.

"Not far."

"As far as we walked the other day?"

"Nothing like that. See those dom palm trees back there? That is where we will camp."

She shrugged at me and picked up one of the bundles. Fine, if she wanted to be stubborn, I would let her. I wouldn't beg her to wrap her feet, which was probably what she was hoping for. We walked in silence to the place I had indicated. When we got there, Nef dropped her bundle and looked around.

"We are sleeping here?" she asked.

"Yes, looks like a good spot."

It was far enough back from the river that we didn't need to worry about crocodiles over night. Other than the dom palms, there wasn't any vegetation taller than knee high, so not much cover from breezes, but it would do.

"But..." Nef gestured at the surrounding area. "Here?"

"Yes, here. What were you expecting?"

"Well, a village. Houses. A chamber for Seti and I to share. A roof, at least. Are we to sleep outside on the ground?"

"We will be sleeping outside a lot while we travel. You will get used to it. I am going to hunt for some dinner. You and Seti can clear a spot for a fire. Do you know how to do that?"

She looked at me blankly.

"But we don't have any beds," she said. "We don't even have bed mats. There is nowhere to bathe, and—"

Her face crumpled and her breathing was shaky. I crouched down in front of her.

"Nef, I know this is a lot of change. I know it is scary. Things are going to be very different from now on. Once we get to where we are going, we will have a house and bed mats and somewhere to bathe. I cannot promise that you and Seti will have a chamber to yourselves. We might have to share one, the three of us. The common people don't usually have houses big enough for separate chambers."

"Will we at least have servants?" she asked, a little tearfully.

"No, I am certain we won't have any servants. You and Seti are going to learn to do things for yourselves. Starting with making a fire. Now, you need a spot that is clear of vegetation. Watch you don't have any overhanging trees either. The sparks from the fire might set them alight. Just pick a spot and clear it down to the dirt. Then find some rocks, about the size of this one here, and lay them out in a circle. Got it? If you can do that much while I am hunting, I will tell you what to do next when I get back."

Nef stared down at the ground and I wasn't sure she was even listening. Frustration welled within me. I had told them there would be no more palaces or servants and I didn't know how else to make them understand. But perhaps I was being unfair. They were only children. I had never had much to do with children and didn't know at what age I could expect them to understand such a change in their circumstances. Perhaps they were just too young.

Hoping to catch a duck, I headed back towards the river, but a hare darted across my path. Better to track the animal I knew was here than spend time searching for a duck that mightn't be. I had thought that if I could feed them duck cooked over coals, it might cheer them a little and belatedly remembered Seti saying she didn't like roasted duck. Well, she might have to learn to like it. The hare was fast, and I tracked it for a while before I took it down with a thrown dagger.

When I returned, the princesses had followed my instructions well enough. They had cleared a spot for a fire and set a ring of stones around it. It was perhaps not as big as I would have made it myself, but it was good enough. They gave me hesitant looks, as if expecting criticism.

"Well done," I said. "Now we need wood for the fire. Lots of little bits of kindling first. Dry grass or leaves, little twigs. Then we need sticks in a range of sizes. Some smaller ones and some bigger." I held up my catch to show them. "Who wants to learn how to skin a hare?"

They both blanched.

"I think we will find the sticks," Nef said.

"And what would you do if I wasn't here?" I asked. "If something happens to me, you will need to know this sort of thing."

"If you weren't here, we wouldn't have caught the hare anyway," she pointed out.

"I will teach you that, too, but for now, one of you is going to learn to prepare the hare for cooking."

Nef shook her head.

"No way," she said. "I am not cutting open a dead animal."

"Me either," Seti said.

I tossed the hare onto the grass.

"Don't bother with a fire, then. We don't need one if we have nothing to cook."

"But—" Nef looked from me to the hare. "You can gut it."

I shook my head.

"I will be fine with a couple of onions," I said. "And I found some duck eggs this morning. That will be enough for me."

"You need to cook the eggs," she said. "We still need a fire for that."

"I am not bothering with a fire to cook an egg. I will eat it raw."

"Eww."

I shrugged at her. "I am the one eating it, so it shouldn't matter to you."

"But what about Seti and me?"

I gestured to the bundle that held our meagre provisions.

"You know where the food is. You can fix your own meal."

"But you promised us a hot dinner," she said.

I exhaled sharply and closed my eyes for a moment, trying to calm myself.

"What do you want from me, Nef? I have told you I am trying to protect you. That includes teaching you how to look after yourselves. I am not your servant and I will not do everything for you. As far as anyone we meet along the way is concerned, I am your mother and you need to start acting like that."

"We had a mother," she said. "And it is not you."

I sighed. That came out all wrong.

"I know I am not your mother, but we need a cover story. Something to tell anyone who wants to know who we are and where we are travelling. The most logical explanation is that we three are together because I am your mother."

She shook her head and looked like she was about to cry.

"Look, we can talk about the cover story later," I said. "There is more to it that I need to explain to you. But for now, are we going to have a hot dinner or not? I won't do things for you just because you refuse to learn. So if you want something hot to eat, one of you is going to learn to skin the hare. If not, I will take it down to the river and throw it in. Having a dead animal lying here all night will attract attention we don't need while we are sleeping."

"I will do it," Seti said. "I want a hot dinner."

She had been silent while Nef and I argued.

"Good, Seti," I said. "Grab the hare and follow me. Nef, have the fuel for the fire ready when we get back."

THIRTEEN
SETI

Tey walked away. I waited to see if she would change her mind, but she was too mean for that. I reached for the dead hare, but didn't know how to pick it up. After a few moments of consideration, I grabbed its ears. They were warm and I gagged a little. Tey walked quite a long way from Nef and the fire before she stopped. My feet were already sore again.

"Here is good," she said. "There are going to be some bits of the hare we don't want to keep, and we will bury those so they don't attract predators overnight. You want to do this a little away from your campsite. There might be blood splatters or you might not bury the remains deep enough and something will come sniffing around."

"What kind of something?" I asked.

"Jackals, wild cats, cobras. You don't want creatures like that sneaking around your camp while you sleep. Understand?"

I swallowed hard and nodded. We needed guards. They would watch for wild animals during the night. I wouldn't be able to sleep for knowing something might be sneaking up on me.

"Good," Tey said. "Now grab a stick, a nice strong one like this, and help me dig a hole. That is right, just there."

We dug a hole together. The ground was harder than I expected and my stick broke. I waited for Tey to get me another, but she only gave me a mean look. So I found a stick and kept digging. When she decided the hole was big enough, she handed me a dagger and showed me how to hold the hare. Then she told me how to get its insides out. I had thought she would do it and I would just watch, but she made me do it all myself.

The inside of the hare was hot and it smelled bad. I gagged and tried to breathe through my mouth. I had never smelled anything so horrible, even when we went to the House of Life to learn about what the embalmers did. Tey showed me which bits to keep and which ones to toss into the hole we dug. We didn't have anything to carry the bits in, so she held the hare's heart and liver and kidneys in her own hands. Blood dripped from between her fingers, but she didn't seem to notice.

I had blood all the way up to my elbows and it even splattered on the front of my gown. I hoped Tey would let me wash my hands. I wouldn't be able to sleep with blood all over me.

I got all the insides out of the hare, even the long windy bit that was like a giant worm, and Tey showed me how to strip off its skin. That took a long time and it was hard to do. Tey just waited and held the inside bits and didn't offer to help me at all. Once I finally got all the skin off, we pushed dirt back into the hole to cover up the skin and guts. Then we took the hare and the rest of its insides back to Nef. She was sitting beside the stone ring, a pile of sticks at her feet.

"I would have tried to light it," she said as we approached. "But I didn't know how."

She eyed the handfuls of meat we carried.

"You need a bowl," she said. "There is the one that had the dates in it."

She found the bowl and set it beside the fire pit. I dropped in the hare and Tey added the inside bits.

"I need to wash my hands," I said, holding them up to show her how bloody they were.

"Me too," Tey said. "We will go down to the river and clean up. Nef, I will show you how to light the fire when we get back."

We walked back to the river. I still hadn't wrapped my feet and they were getting pretty sore with all this walking.

"Stay right on the bank," Tey said. "You don't know what is lurking in the water, especially in the dark. If you go out too far, you might find something grabbing you by the leg to drag you in."

I stopped at the water's edge and crouched to wash my arms. I would have liked to take off my gown and wash it again, but Tey seemed to be in a hurry. Maybe she was hungry. I was too, so I didn't suggest we stay to wash my gown.

My feet were very sore by the time we headed back to Nef. I should have washed them while we were at the river, but I had only been thinking about getting the blood off my hands.

"Are your feet hurting again?" Tey asked.

"No," I said.

She walked a little further, then she stopped and sighed.

"Seti, when you hurt yourself, I need you to tell me so we can do something about it."

"What can you do, though?" I asked. "I need shoes."

"I will get you shoes at the next village we stop at. For now, you can wrap your feet again."

I shrugged and didn't say anything else.

When we got back to Nef, Tey showed us how to make a fire using some sticks and kindling. Maybe she wasn't feeling as mean as usual because she started the fire herself instead of making us do it. She did make us chop the dead hare into chunks with one of her daggers, though, and poke sticks through them. Then we had to set them in the ring of stones, just beside the flames but not in them, so they wouldn't burn.

I was so hungry I could hardly think by then. The sun hovered just a little above the horizon and I supposed washing my hands earlier would be all the bath I would get tonight. I didn't really feel like walking all the way back to the river again anyway. I settled back on my heels, enjoying the heat of the fire on my face and the smell of the roasting meat. At least now we could relax after two days of travelling.

But of course Tey wouldn't let us sit and rest.

"While that is cooking, I want to show you a few things," she said. "Basic moves you can use if you need to defend yourselves."

Nef shrugged as if to say she didn't care, but she stood up.

"Seti, get up," Tey said.

"I am tired," I said.

"You can sleep after we eat. I am going to teach you something while the hare cooks."

"I already learnt how to gut it. That is enough for tonight."

I stared straight into the fire and didn't let myself look at her. I could tell from her voice she was feeling mean again.

"Seti, if the bad men find us, you need to be able to defend yourself," Tey said.

"I am too little. They will be so much bigger than me, they will capture me anyway. Then they will probably kill me and I won't need to know anything."

"Just because someone is bigger than you, doesn't mean you cannot fight back," Tey said. "Your advantage is that you are small and fast. If the bad men come, you need to surprise them, then you can run away. It is not about taking down someone who is much bigger than you. It is about distracting them to give yourself time to get away."

"But I am too tired," I said. "The bad men won't come tonight."

"They could come at any time. You need to be prepared."

"If the bad men find us, doesn't that mean you didn't do a good enough job? Since you're supposed to protect us and everything."

Tey inhaled and exhaled loudly. I ignored her and kept looking into the fire. Its heat was nice and I started to get quite sleepy, despite my stomach being so empty it hurt.

Then something grabbed me from behind and knocked me to the ground. Before I could even figure out what had happened, Tey had one knee on my chest and her dagger pressed against my throat. My heart raced and my hands were shaking. I huffed at her.

"Tey, you scared me."

"If I was a bad man, you would be dead already," she said.

"Well, you're not a bad man and that was mean."

She pressed the tip of her dagger into my neck. It stung, and I was sure I felt blood running down my throat. I got a bit scared. Maybe she really was going to kill us after all.

"What are you doing?" I asked. My voice came out all squeaky.

"Are you ready to learn?"

"Get off me."

"Do you see how easy it would be for someone to kill you when you know nothing about how to defend yourself?" she asked.

FOURTEEN
TEY

"I said get off me," Seti said.

Her face had gone red and she glared up at me. From the corner of my eye, I noticed Nef creeping towards us.

"Stay out of this, Nef," I said.

She stopped.

Wind swirled around us, kicking up handfuls of sand which scraped across my skin. The fire crackled and the flames leaped. A sandstorm, perhaps? I had experienced them twice while training in the desert and had no more shelter then than we did now. I removed my dagger from Seti's throat and got to my feet. If we were about to face a sandstorm, it was more important that we did what we could to prepare than that I continued her lesson. We needed to put out the fire, for starters.

But the breeze settled and the sand lay still again. Not a sand-storm, just a few gusts of wind. I turned back to Seti, who was now sitting up.

"Seti, you need to learn how to protect yourself," I said. "Let me teach you one move tonight. That is all. Then tomorrow you can learn another. By the time we get to where we are going, you will know a range of techniques that will help you if the bad men find us."

I held out my hand to help her up. She considered me with a frown.

"I don't like you putting your dagger to my throat," she said. "That was mean."

"I wasn't trying to be mean. I was trying to show you how quickly things can go wrong, especially when you know nothing about how to defend yourself."

"I don't want you to do that again."

"I won't if you get up and learn."

She glowered at me for a few moments.

"Promise?" she asked at last.

I shrugged and she seemed to take that as adequate confirmation. She reached for my hand and I hauled her to her feet.

"Right, this is a move you can use if someone comes up from behind and grabs you," I said. "Nef, let's start with you. Come stand here in front of me. That is right, just there. Turn around so your back is to me. Now I am going to put my arm around your neck."

By the time the hare was ready, both girls had practised escaping my grip. Nef caught on quickly and seemed to relish our practice. Seti was more hesitant, still convinced she was too small to defend herself.

"That is enough for now," I said. "We can practice some more tomorrow and I will teach you another move. Let's eat now."

I placed the duck eggs right at the edge of the fire so they could cook while we ate the hare off the sticks. It was a little tough, but it was hot and tasty.

"It is actually pretty good," Nef said. Juice dripped down her hands and she licked it off.

"I promised you a hot dinner," I said.

She stared down at the remains of her share of the hare and seemed to be thinking very hard. At last, she looked back up at me.

"Tey, we haven't thanked you yet. For looking after us. You left your family to take us away so the bad men won't get us."

An unexpected surge of emotion flooded me.

"You are welcome." I didn't know what else to say.

"Why did you do it?" she asked. "You don't even know us."

I shrugged, not wanting to share my reasons.

"Is it because you know our sister?" she pressed.

"My brother is the captain of her personal squad," I said. "But I have never met her myself."

"So why then?"

I stared into the fire while I tried to find the right words. This was a conversation we had to have sooner or later. May as well get it over with.

"Do you know what is expected of the common women?" I asked. "Once they reach a certain age?"

Nef shrugged. "They get married."

"Yes, marriage. Children. Keeping the house clean, brewing beer, baking bread. A woman becomes a servant to her husband and his children."

"So?" Nef asked.

"So I didn't want that. I wanted to choose my own life. I wanted... something else. Something more."

"Seti and I have to get married, too." Nef spoke slowly, as if trying to explain something to a very dimwitted child. "We are supposed to have important marriages. Strategic alliances."

"Yes, your marriages would have been very different to mine. You would have servants to do all the things a common woman spends her day doing. But just like me, you had no say in your future."

"We are expected to be useful to Pharaoh," she said. "It is our purpose to have important marriages."

"But that is not what I want," I said. "I don't want to marry. I don't want to be tied to a man or his house or his children."

Nef looked at me blankly.

"So, what do you want, then?" she asked.

I sighed and stared into the fire for a while. My father had asked the same thing once and I hadn't known how to answer him. I wasn't sure I knew even now.

"Something more," I said. "I want to do things. See things. Be somebody."

"I don't understand," Nef said.

"That is all right," I said. "Nobody ever does."

We were silent as we finished our meal. I couldn't guess what the princesses were thinking about. They had been through a lot over the last two days and they obviously hadn't made up their minds about me yet. I didn't expect them to love me — I didn't want to replace their mother, despite our cover story — but I hoped that with time they might consider me a friend. We were going to be together for a good long while. It was Nef who broke the silence.

"Tey?" she asked. "Where are we going?"

"To Nubet. Do you know where that is?"

"We learnt a little about geography in our lessons. I think it is way down to the south."

"That is right. It is a long way from here. We need to keep travelling down the Great River. We will go past Thebes and even past Behdet."

"Is it near Nubia?" Seti asked.

"Yes, Seti," I said. "Well done. Nubia is to our south. We aren't going quite that far, but we will be close."

"Why are we going to Nubet?" Nef asked.

"I think I know," Seti said. "It is so she doesn't have to get married."

"Because it is a long way from Akhetaten," I said. "And because there is nothing to connect you to that place. No reason for anyone to think you might travel there."

"Does that mean we won't get married either?" Seti asked.

"You are a little young to worry about that," I said. "When you are old enough, I suppose you can choose for yourself whether you marry or not."

"Of course we will," Nef said. "Princesses always get married. But who will find our husbands for us?"

Of all the concerns I had thought they might have, husbands was not one of them.

"We will figure that out when the time comes," I said.

"Do you know someone there?" Nef asked. "In Nubet?"

"No, but that doesn't matter. As long as we stick together, we will be fine. Now, you both need to learn our cover story. If anyone asks who you are or where we are going, this is what you tell them. My name is Tentamun. You will call me Mother, but other people will call me Ten. Nef, your new name will be Nebetia and we will call you Neb. Seti, you will be Senseneb or Sensen for short. Can you remember that?"

"Why do we need new names?" Seti asked. "I like my name."

"If anyone is asking around about two princesses who have disappeared, and they hear about two girls who have the same names as you, don't you think they will come looking for you? They will want to make sure you aren't the princesses they are searching for."

"But we are the princesses," Seti said.

"Yes, but you can never tell anyone that. We have to disappear. We cannot risk someone overhearing us using your old names, so from now on, you are Neb and Sensen, and I am Mother. Understood?"

"I don't want to," Seti said.

"There are going to be lots of things you don't want to do," I said. "You will have to do them anyway. Now, if anyone asks where we are going, you can tell them Nubet."

"But won't that mean they might tell other people we are going to Nubet?" Nef asked.

"That is right, Neb. Why won't it matter if we tell people where we are really going?"

She thought for a few moments.

"Oh, because nobody knows our real names," she said. "They will only know we are Neb and Sensen and we are going to Nubet."

"That is right. Neb and Sensen are sisters. Your father, my husband, has gone to the West. He used to work in one of

Pharaoh's construction teams. He was building a temple for Aten, but he got killed at work. Do you think you can remember that?"

"Uh huh," Nef said.

"Sensen, are you keeping up?" I asked.

"I don't want to be Sensen," Seti said.

"Do you want a different name?" I asked. "You can choose for yourself. You don't have to be Sensen."

"No, I want to be Seti. I have always been Seti."

I restrained my sigh.

"Let's talk about that some more later," I said. "Since your father died, we have been left destitute. Everything we had went to pay off his debts and we have nothing left. The only family we have left alive is his mother, your grandmother, who lives in Nubet."

"You said you didn't know anyone in Nubet," Nef said.

"It is a cover story, Neb. We need a reason to go there. If we don't expect to find someone we know, why would we travel halfway across the country? We would have stayed where we were."

"Do we tell people we are from Akhetaten?" she asked.

I had changed my mind about this a couple of times. I worried it might create a connection someone would want to investigate, but our story was complicated enough. The more they had to remember, the more likely they would slip up. Anyone searching for the princesses would likely assume they were secreted out of town, but would expect them to be travelling with guards. And guards were always male. Two girls travelling with their destitute mother would be neither suspicious nor memorable.

"Yes," I said. "If anyone asks where we came from, you can say Akhetaten."

"If we can say we are from Akhetaten, I want to be Seti," Seti said.

"Later, Sensen," I said. "The woman we are travelling to, your grandmother, her name is Henuttaneb. Can you remember that?"

"Henuttaneb," Nef repeated obediently.

"Sensen?"

She pouted. I raised my eyebrows and waited.

"Henuttaneb," she muttered.

"Good. Now, tell me our cover story. You go first, Neb. What is your name?"

"Neb, and that is my sister, Senseneb, but we call her Sensen, and you are our mother."

"What is my name?"

"Ten."

I nodded. "Go on."

"We are from Akhetaten. Our father was killed building a temple for Pharaoh and we are going to our grandmother because she is the only family we have. She lives in Nubet and we are going to live with her."

"Good job," I said. "Your turn, Sensen."

"But what if they ask me questions?" Nef asked.

"Just say you don't remember."

The fire was dying down a little, so I leaned forward to poke another stick into it.

"But what if they keep asking and they want an answer?" she asked.

"Can you cry if you have to? You could burst into tears and say you miss your father."

"I do miss my father," she said, very quietly.

I suddenly realised it had only been a couple of weeks since their father, the great Pharaoh Akhenaten, had gone to the West. They were still grieving and now they had been uprooted. Taken away from everything they knew, everyone they loved. Cast out of their home with someone who was a stranger. Maybe I was expecting too much of them.

"This must be difficult for you," I said. "It is a lot of change in a very short time."

"Do you think our sister loves us?" Nef asked and her voice trembled.

"Of course she does. Why do you ask?"

She shrugged and looked away.

"I thought maybe she hated us. That we annoy her or something. So she sent us away to get rid of us."

"Neb, your sister loves you very much. She sent you away to keep you safe. She knew you were in terrible danger in Akhetaten."

"From the bad men," Nef said.

"Yes, the bad men. She didn't want them to find you, so she asked my brother to find someone who could take you far away and keep you safe."

"And we can really never go home again?"

"I am sorry, but no. If you go back, the bad men will find you. And it is not just the two of you we are protecting. If they find out where you are, your sister is also in danger. There can only be one queen and there are people who would kill your sister so they can make one of you queen. There are also people who would kill both of you to make sure nobody else can make you queen. It is all terribly complicated, but do you understand that if you stayed there, all three of you would be in danger?"

"Sort of."

"Good," I said. "Now, Sensen, it is your turn. Tell me our story."

"My name is Seti," she said.

I would fight that battle tomorrow. Perhaps once she had had some sleep and time to think, she would understand why she had to change her name.

"What is the rest of the story?" I asked.

"Father is dead and we have to go to his mother to live with her," Seti said.

I prodded her for more detail and she was able to tell me most of the story. Neither girl could remember their "grandmother's" name, but I figured it wasn't important. Nobody would expect girls of their age to remember a detail like that, considering they had probably only ever heard her referred to as Grandmother, or perhaps as Mother by their father.

"Once more," I said. "Then let's get some sleep. Neb, tell me our story."

FIFTEEN
TEY

I slept restlessly and dreamed I woke to find the princesses gone. When I really woke, with my heart pounding so loudly that I wouldn't have heard anyone approaching us, they were fast asleep, huddled together under their shawls and the linen sheets. I would have to get proper blankets for them. My cloak kept me warm enough, but they looked cold.

I must have fallen asleep again and woke shortly after dawn when a flock of birds rose into the air, screeching as if startled. I slid a dagger from its sheath on my forearm and slowly pushed my cloak aside. Nef was already awake, sitting with her sheet wrapped around her shoulders. Seti seemed to have woken at the same time as me.

"Tey?" Nef's gaze went straight to the dagger in my hand.

"Shh."

I could see no sign of danger around us and could hear nothing other than the fading squawks and the breeze rustling a nearby bush. An insect buzzed by my ear. I got to my feet, still scanning our surroundings. Movement in the tall grasses to our left.

"Get up," I said. "If I tell you to run, go straight to the boat. Untie the rope and be ready to go. I will follow as soon as I can."

"Where are you going?" Nef asked.

I stalked towards the grasses. They waved in the breeze. I listened hard, but heard nothing that seemed out of place. I crept closer, my dagger ready.

"You may as well come out now," I said. "If I have to go in there, I will stab first and ask questions later, if you live that long."

No response.

The grasses continued to shift in the breeze. Somewhere behind me, a lone bird squawked. The breeze might be enough to cover the sound of a man trying to be very quiet, but this close to his hiding place, I should be able to hear him breathing. But I heard nothing other than the wind and the grasses and the bird.

I flung myself into the grasses, ready to stab my dagger into any living body I encountered. But nobody was there. I felt foolish as I got to my feet. I searched the perimeter of our campsite for any sign someone had been nearby. No footprints, no broken branches or disturbed grasses. Nobody had been here other than us.

I returned to the princesses, who stood side by side holding hands. Their faces were white and Seti had been crying.

"Time to go," I said.

"You didn't find him?" Nef asked, her voice very quiet.

I hesitated. Was it better to say I had been mistaken about somebody spying on us or to let them think he had escaped? I couldn't decide quickly enough.

"Grab your things," I said instead.

I had never seen them move so fast as they snatched up the linen cloths and bundled our remaining supplies. In the time it took me to kick dirt over the lingering coals, they were ready to go. We hurried down to the boat, threw in our things, and were out on the water in a matter of minutes. I raised the sail and the boat shot off.

"You can eat if you're hungry," I said. "Seti, show me your feet."

She hadn't had time to wrap them before we left.

Seti raised one foot to show me the underside. The cut on the bottom had opened again, but other than a bit of dirt, her feet looked sound enough.

"Are the bad men following us?" Nef asked. "Can you see them?"

"No, I don't think anyone is nearby right now," I said. "We are moving too fast for someone to keep up on the shore, so they would have to follow in a boat and while we are on this straight stretch of the river, we would see them. You are safe."

Her face was doubtful, but she didn't push me. We shared the last of the dates and vegetables, and the princesses talked quietly amongst themselves while I focussed on the boat. An hour or so later, Nef asked if we could go ashore.

"I don't want to do it in the boat again, because then I will have to wash my dress," she said. "And I cannot hold it any longer. I didn't have time to go before we left."

"We can stop briefly," I said. "But we cannot stay for long if we want to reach the next village before dark. We will find somewhere near the village to sleep and I will go for supplies in the morning. Seti cannot go much longer without shoes."

I could do with a change of clothes myself. My hands were the only part of me that had been washed since we left Akhetaten. I manoeuvred the boat over to the shore and felt a glimmer of pride when Nef secured it without being asked. They were learning to work with me.

The girls went off behind some shrubs to do their business. There was no sign of anyone nearby and I would hear them if there was a problem. I crouched on the riverbank to relieve myself. As I stood, a nearby bush rustled. Still adjusting my skirt, I snatched a dagger from the sheath on my calf. It was probably nothing again, but I couldn't afford to find I didn't have a weapon in my hand when I needed it.

I stalked over to the bushes. They rustled again and I spotted a silhouette in their midst. I flung myself at him without hesitation. He had started to stand and his belly was an easy target for my dagger. I moved so quickly he never even had time to raise his hands to defend himself.

As he lay dying at my feet, I studied him. He was probably only a year or two older than me. I had expected our pursuers to be much older, but I, of all people, shouldn't assume a person wasn't well trained just because they were young. Look at my brother, Intef. He had been training since he was seven years old and now, at fifteen, his abilities exceeded those of men twice his age.

I checked the man for weapons in case he had anything useful. It was only when I discovered he wasn't carrying even so much as a single dagger that I realised I might have made a mistake. I studied him more carefully. His skin was sun-darkened and his palms were calloused, but not in the way a soldier's would be. If I wasn't mistaken, he was a farmer.

My heart sank. He had probably stumbled on us by accident. Maybe he lived nearby and had come down to the riverbank in search of ducks or eggs or fish. Perhaps this was his farmland we stopped on. I had made a terrible mistake. I hadn't been protecting the princesses from an assassin. I had killed an innocent man. My stomach rolled and my mouth tasted bitter. I swallowed hard, not wanting to vomit in front of the princesses.

"Tey?" Nef called.

The man was dead. There was nothing I could do to save him. I pulled his body out from the bushes and laid him out. If someone came looking for him, they would find him.

"I am sorry," I whispered.

Then I hurried back to the princesses.

"Let's go," I said. "Back to the boat."

"Was it one of the bad men?" Seti asked.

"Yes, it was a bad man. You don't need to fear him, though. He is dead. He won't be coming after us again. But we need to leave now in case he has friends with him."

Or in case someone came looking for him, wondering why he hadn't returned home yet.

The princesses were silent as we headed back out into the middle of the river. It was only after we caught the wind that Nef spoke.

"Are you sure he was dead? Really sure?"

"I am."

I couldn't look at her. Didn't want either of them to see my guilt. It was my job to protect them and I did what I thought was necessary. But I acted too hastily. A man was dead because I misjudged the situation.

SIXTEEN

TEY

The day was already warm, but our passage along the river kept us cool enough. The princesses were quiet as we sailed, likely shocked by this morning's events. My own emotions were all over the place. I was mad at myself for being too hasty. For making the wrong decision. I was sorry for the man, and his family, and whoever found him lying there. I feared someone might have seen us, or would see us sailing past, and put the pieces together. We could soon have people hunting us for more reason than just the missing princesses.

I buried my guilt and the gnawing edge of fear with the reminder that I was charged with keeping the princesses safe. There hadn't been time to establish the man's intentions. Whatever he had been going to do, whoever he was, he was hiding and spying on us. That alone was reason enough for suspicion.

I distracted myself by making the princesses repeat our cover story a few times. Seti still objected to changing her name, but eventually conceded she would use Sensen when there were other people around to hear, as long as we still called her Seti in private. I wasn't happy with the idea — they were more likely to slip up and use the wrong name — but at least it stopped our argument, so I agreed we would only use our cover names in public.

We camped onshore again, although I would have preferred to sail through the night. We were safe out on the water. But we were out of supplies and Seti had been moaning about being hungry for at least an hour. I caught a duck and this time it was Nef who learnt to disembowel it. Seti helped her pluck the feathers. Then I taught them another move they could use to escape someone trying to grab them. I didn't make them work very hard, but when I said we had finished, they flung themselves on the ground with exaggerated sighs of relief.

As we waited for the duck to cook, the princesses still seemed subdued. If they were more afraid now they had seen me kill a man, that was a good thing. Fear kept you alert and alive. Complacency could get you killed.

"Tey, do you miss your family?" Nef asked.

The fire flared a little too high and I adjusted the burning wood, giving myself time to think. I wasn't sure how much I wanted to tell them about my previous life. The flames crackled as it settled again and the meaty aroma of roasting duck made my stomach rumble and my mouth water.

"I do," I said at last. "I miss Papa and my brother."

"What about your mother?" she asked.

"She went to the West many years ago," I said. "She died giving birth to our sister. I barely remember her."

"Oh." Nef was quiet for a while. "Our mother died from the plague, but our sisters Merytaten and Meketaten died giving birth."

"Don't forget Nefer," Seti said quietly. "The plague got her too."

We had all known grief and the loss of a sister. Perhaps that might give me a way to bond with them.

"I miss our sister and our brother," Nef said. "I miss the palace and hot baths. Servants. Soft beds. Having lots of food. Being able to change my clothes whenever I want."

"You know you won't have servants or palaces again," I said. "But once we get to Nubet, we will find a place to live. You will have hot baths again, although you will have to fetch the water and heat it yourself. We will have beds and food and extra clothes. It won't be so bad. You will see."

"But don't you miss those things too?" she asked, very earnestly as if she truly wanted to understand. "You haven't once said you wanted more food or a house or anything."

"This is temporary," I said. "We will not live like this forever. Besides, my life was very different to yours. I didn't live in a palace and have servants to bring me hot water or wash my clothes. I had to do things for myself."

There was no point explaining this wasn't all that different to how I trained myself. By going without food or shelter. By forcing myself to survive on nothing but what I could scavenge or could kill with my dagger. They wouldn't understand I did it to make myself stronger. More self sufficient. Better able to cope, even though I didn't know at the time what I was preparing myself for, just that the day would come when I would *do* something. They seemed to view our current situation as a trial. Something to suffer or endure. I could live like this for the rest of my life if I had to. It was Seti who dragged me from my thoughts this time.

"Are we going home tomorrow?" she asked.

I chose my words carefully.

"We cannot go home. I have explained this before. There are bad men there who want to kill you. I am taking you somewhere you will be safe."

"But how long?" she asked. "When will we be able to go home? I want to see Ankhesenpaaten, and Tutankhaten will wonder why we have stopped visiting him."

"That is our little brother," Nef said in an aside to me. "He is very young and also sickly. Nobody thinks he will live long enough to grow up."

"Your sister entrusted you to me," I said. "It is my job to look after you. It will be just the three of us from now on."

"But I want to go home." Seti's voice rose, both in pitch and volume.

Sand swirled around us. This had also happened the last time

Seti got upset. It would be an unlikely coincidence — the sudden development of what seemed to be a sandstorm each time she was unhappy — which made me wonder whether she somehow made it happen. I had never heard of such an ability before, but there was much I didn't know. Perhaps Seti didn't even know she was doing it, or maybe she had no control over it. If she got worked up enough, how bad would it get? I didn't particularly want to find out. Maybe if I could get her to calm down, it would stop.

"Seti, take a deep breath for me," I said. "That is it, and another."

The sand dropped to the ground. Interesting it stopped as soon as she calmed. I would have to keep an eye on this.

"Good girl," I said. "Now let's think about what sort of supplies we need. Can you help me make a list? We should reach a village tomorrow or the next day at the latest."

SEVENTEEN

SETI

I had trouble sleeping that night. My back was sore from sitting in the boat all day, I was sick of sleeping outside on the ground and I wanted to go home. I cracked open my eyes to see where Tey was. She was sitting on the other side of the fire. The flames were making a lot of crackling and hissing and popping, and she wouldn't hear us if we were quiet.

"Nef, are you awake?" I whispered.

"Sort of," she said in a sleepy voice.

"I think we should run away. We can wait until Tey goes to sleep and then sneak off. We can find someone and tell them we are princesses. They will have to take us home if we tell them to."

Nef was quiet for a long time and I thought she had gone to sleep.

"Seti, we cannot go home," she said. "Have you not been listening to Tey?"

"I know she says there are bad men looking for us, but that is only because we left, and she already killed the bad man anyway. If we went home, Ankhesenpaaten would tell the army to keep us safe. We could stay inside the palace. There are soldiers at every door. Nobody can kill us there."

"I think Ankhesenpaaten thinks the bad men might be inside

the palace," Nef said. "If she thought it was safe for us to stay, she wouldn't have let her captain take us away."

"But she wouldn't have sent us away if she knew we would have to sleep outside. I would rather be locked in our bedchamber than spend all day in a boat and sleep on the ground. I want a bath and a hot dinner."

"We had a hot dinner, Seti. And I guess we can bathe in the river when we need to."

"You sound like you like it."

I didn't mean to sound like I was accusing her of something bad, but I didn't like that Nef seemed to enjoy living like this. We were princesses. We were supposed to live in a palace. With servants and soft beds and hot dinners we didn't have to cut the insides out of ourselves.

"I didn't say I liked it, but I would rather live like this than be dead," Nef said.

"Ankhesenpaaten wouldn't let anyone make us dead," I said, rather grumpily.

I rolled over so my back was to her. There was no point talking to Nef. She didn't understand anything.

EIGHTEEN

TEY

We came across a village the following day, much larger than the small cluster of houses I stole the vegetables from. I didn't want to risk stealing again. The more I did it, the more chance of being caught, and what would happen to the princesses if I was arrested? I found a secluded place on the riverbank where they could wait for me.

"I might be gone all day," I said. "I need you to stay here and not wander off."

"Can we come?" Nef asked. "Wouldn't we be safer with you?"

"I don't want anyone to see you," I said. "If people see a lone woman from time to time, nobody who is searching for you will think anything of it. If they see you with me, people will be more likely to think of us if someone asks about two missing girls. The more we have to use our cover story, the more likely it will reach someone who starts asking questions."

"Why will it take you so long to get supplies?" she asked. "We already told you what to get."

"I have nothing to trade except my daggers and I need those to keep you safe." I wouldn't use my mother's ring and I didn't want to waste their gems. "I will have to find some work for the day.

Once I have my wages — barley probably — I can trade that for what we need. I will be back as soon as I can."

"What if you don't come back?" she asked.

Nef was right. This was a discussion we needed to have. It had been playing on my mind as we sailed, but I didn't have an answer yet. I must have taken too long to reply as Nef came up with her own answer.

"When the bad men find us," she said, "if you aren't here to protect us, they will kill us."

I glanced from her to Seti. How much did Seti understand? She acted so much younger than Nef, although they had told me there was only two years between them. She had just turned seven and Nef was almost nine. I crouched so I was at eye level with both of them.

"If I don't come back, go to Akhetaten and find my brother," I said. "His name is Intef. If you can get to him, he will protect you."

"He isn't one of the bad men?" Seti asked, a little tearfully.

"Don't you remember Intef?" I asked. "He is the captain of your sister's personal squad, the soldiers who protect her. He brought you to me and told me to keep you safe from the bad men."

"He took us away from Ankhesenpaaten," she said. "I was crying and he picked me up and wouldn't let me go back to her."

"Seti, he told her he was taking us and she let him," Nef said. "She didn't tell him to stop. So I think she trusts him."

"She does trust him," I said. "If something happens to me, he will protect you. But Akhetaten is a long way from here and you would have to get all the way back by yourselves."

I had hoped they might offer a suggestion on how they would do that, but they just looked at me. It was hard not to compare them to myself at that age. Most children didn't know how to kill a man. Papa taught me to wield a dagger when I was very young, perhaps no more than three or four years old, and by the time I was six, I was passably proficient in basic defence skills. For several years after that, Papa refused to teach me any more. He considered it acceptable for a girl to know how to defend herself, which showed what an extraordinary man he was, but he refused to accept that a girl could learn to attack.

I was ten years old before he agreed to teach me more, and that was only because I came home with a bloodied nose and two black eyes after picking a fight with an older boy to learn the skills I wanted. My father said then he thought I would have been happier if I had been born a boy. He said other girls — ordinary girls — didn't want to know how to kill a man. Perhaps I was expecting too much from the princesses.

"If I am not back by the time the sun sets, I want you to take the boat and leave. You will need to row yourselves out to where you can catch the current, but then you just need to keep the boat steady. The current will take you all the way back to Akhetaten as long as you don't put the sail up. The wharf is right in front of the palace, but don't stop at the jetties where everyone will see you. Stop a little before it if you can and stay out of sight. Go around to the west entrance, where Intef brought you out to me. Do you remember where that is? Go inside and find Intef. He will keep you safe."

Nef nodded again, although from the way her forehead wrinkled, I figured she was unsure.

"Say it back to me," I said. "Tell me the plan."

Once she had repeated it accurately, I stood and placed my hand on her shoulder.

"You are the oldest, Nef. You need to look after Seti. Keep out of sight and if anyone comes near you, stay very quiet and still. I will be back before sundown."

"And if you don't, we get in the boat and go find Intef," Nef said.

"Good, that is right."

I waited until they were hidden, then walked away, although not without a few backward glances to be sure they definitely weren't visible. I wasn't sure I was doing the right thing in leaving them alone all day, but I couldn't think of any other solution.

NINETEEN
TEY

I had feared it mightn't be easy to find a day's work in a village of this size, but I arrived to discover they had started the harvest the day before. There was plenty of work to be done and I quickly found a farmer who was happy to give me a bag of barley for my labour in his field. He was so desperate for help, he didn't even care I was a woman. He asked no questions, so I had no reason to use our cover story, although I did tell him my name was Tentamun.

I spent the day picking onions. This was not something my training prepared me for, and the day was only half over before my back ached. I could run for hours, even in the middle of the harvest season of *shemu*. I could climb rocky cliffs with nothing but my hands and feet. I could track and hunt and find water, but none of those things pained me like spending all day crouched in a field.

My fellow workers weren't particularly friendly, although whether it was because they were too intent on their own work or they were suspicious of strangers, I wasn't sure. It was fine with me if they didn't want to chat. The fewer people I had to explain our journey to, the better. I caught one of them staring at me from time to time, but kept my head down and pretended I didn't see him.

It wasn't until we had finished for the day and I received my bag of barley that the man sidled up and asked where I was from. I felt uneasy and gave him vague answers, not wanting to even use our cover story. It wasn't anything specific apart from the way he didn't look directly at me, but snuck glances when he thought I wasn't looking. Something about him didn't feel right. I made my excuses and left.

I found a small market and some sandals for Seti. The stall owner drove an unnecessarily hard bargain and took far more of my barley than I would have liked. I spent the rest on food, although I couldn't get everything the princesses asked for after buying the sandals. I could hunt to supplement our supplies, though, and maybe I should see if I could get work in the next village as well. While the harvest was in progress, work would be easy to come by and I should take advantage of that while I could.

As I purchased the supplies, I spotted the man who spoke to me earlier. He was some distance away, but stared right at me. I gave him a hard look to let him know I saw him. He looked away and pretended to be interested in something at a nearby stall. I watched him out of the corner of my eye and as I moved on, so did he. He was following me.

I lingered in the market for some time, not wanting to lead him back to the princesses. Every time I thought I had lost him, he would appear again. I had planned to stay the night here and move on in the morning, but maybe it would be better to leave tonight.

The sun was close to setting, filling the sky with orange and purple streaks. I had to get back to the princesses before they put our emergency plan into action. If I waited much longer, I wouldn't reach them before dusk.

I left the market, walking swiftly with my sack of provisions over my shoulder and my other hand free in case I needed a dagger. As I expected, the man followed.

I waited until we were out of sight of the village, then dropped my sack and turned to face him. My dagger was already in my hand. He kept coming towards me, and I knew the moment he spotted my dagger. He hesitated and I thought he might turn back, but he didn't.

He stopped a few paces in front of me.

"Why are you following me?" I asked.

As before, he didn't look me in the eyes.

"I don't have to explain myself to you," he said. "I can walk around my own village."

"I don't like being followed."

He shrugged. "Seems to me there is not much you can do about that."

I casually swung my dagger, bringing his attention back to it.

"How sure about that are you?" I asked. "Perhaps you would like to see what I can do with a dagger? I am quick with it. I could remove your kidney while you are still alive. Of course, you won't live much longer once I have taken it, but I can get in and get it out before you die. Would you like me to demonstrate?"

He took a step or two back.

"Don't be hasty," he said. "You shouldn't be out wandering on your own. Your father know where you are?"

"It is not your business where I choose to go, alone or otherwise."

"No man would be happy to see his daughter working alone in the field all day."

"Plenty of women help their husbands at harvest time."

"Except you are not married to any of the men here," he said.

"Why does that matter to you? I worked as hard as anyone else out there today. I received my pay and now I am leaving."

"Where are you going? There are no houses in that direction."

"That is none of your concern. Now, I am tired after a long day and I would like to be on my way. Are you going to leave me alone, or do I need to show you how fast my dagger is?"

"A respectable woman would not be out walking by herself," he said.

I stepped up to him and rested the point of my dagger against his belly, right at the spot where his kidney was. This close, I could smell his rank odour.

"I am warning you," I said. "I don't want any trouble, but I will not tolerate you following me. Go home and leave me alone."

He smirked a little. Before he could speak, I pressed my dagger in. Not far enough to seriously hurt him, just to poke through his shirt and pierce his skin. He let out a yell and stumbled back, one hand grasping his side as if mortally wounded.

"You cut me," he howled. "What is wrong with you?"

"I warned you. Now leave me alone. If you get close enough for my dagger to touch you again, I *will* carve out your kidney before you have time to fall down."

I grabbed my sack and set off again.

"There is something wrong with you," he called after me. "Unnatural, that is what you are. A woman thinking she can wave a dagger around and stab an innocent man. Someone ought to put you in your place."

I kept walking. When I glanced over my shoulder to make sure he wasn't stupid enough to keep following me, he was stumbling back towards the village. He was not as badly injured as he pretended, but I feared he might cause more trouble. I set off at a jog. I had wasted far too much time with him.

TWENTY

TEY

The sun was very close to setting before I reached the place where the princesses waited.

"Nef," I called softly as I approached. "Seti. It is just me."

For a moment, I feared they may have already gone, but then they emerged from their hiding place.

"We didn't think you were coming," Nef said. Although she spoke calmly enough, tears streaked her face. "We were just about to leave like you said to."

"I am sorry. I got delayed. We need to go, though. It isn't safe to stay here tonight."

"We are going to sleep in the boat again?" Seti sniffled and rubbed her nose with the back of her hand. "I don't want to."

"I had planned to spend the night here, but we cannot. Grab our things. We need to leave."

"I am not going." Seti crossed her arms over her chest and glowered at me.

"Seti, we don't have time for this. We need to go."

"What happened?" Nef asked. "Was one of the bad men there?"

"We just need to leave," I said.

"You are scaring us, Tey," Nef said. "Why do we need to go so fast?"

I had not intended to share any details with them, thinking it would frighten them, but maybe I needed to be honest. Perhaps they would understand better then.

"One of the men I worked with today was a little too interested in me," I said. "He followed me from the village and we had a bit of a fight. He left, but he was injured and I am afraid he might come looking for me again. That is why we cannot stay here tonight."

Nef seemed to grasp the seriousness of the situation, but Seti shook her head.

"I am not going," she announced. "I am sick of being on the boat and I want to go home."

"You know why you cannot go home," I said. "And you know it is important we keep moving so the bad men don't find us."

"Our sister will protect us from the bad men." Seti's voice was far too loud. "She is the queen and she would set the whole army on the bad men if she knew about them."

"Seti, keep your voice down," I said. "Your sister doesn't control the army and she was the one who sent you away, remember? It is my job to keep you safe. Now come on, let's go."

"I said I am not going." Her voice grew louder with each word. "I want to go home."

"Nef, you will have to carry our things." I grabbed Seti's arm and dragged her towards the boat.

"Let me go," she screeched. "My sister is the queen and she will cut off your head."

I pulled Seti in against my chest and clapped my hand over her mouth.

"Seti, be quiet," I said. "We cannot risk people finding out who you are."

She writhed and squealed. If anyone hid nearby, watching us in the dark, they would have already guessed who the girls were. Anyone watching would think I was abducting them.

An eddy of sand swirled around us. Twice before when Seti had gotten upset, I noticed a disturbance in the sand. Before I could wonder any further, lamp light caught my eye. People headed towards us, maybe a dozen or so.

"Nef, get our things," I said. "Quickly."

My voice was terse and she rushed to obey. I picked Seti up and carried her, squirming and kicking, to the boat. It was awkward since I had to keep one hand over her mouth. Nef tossed in our bundles and untied the rope securing it, then I dropped Seti in. As soon as I let her go, she flung herself to the side of the boat, seemingly intent on tossing herself overboard. Nef managed to climb in as the boat rocked from side to side.

"Nef, you will have to row," I said as I grabbed Seti's leg. "Quickly now. There are people coming and I don't want to be here to find out why."

Nef fumbled for the oars. Her hands shook and she didn't seem to know what to do. I tried to hold Seti with one arm so I could help, but she wriggled too much. The boat would tip over if she didn't settle. I pressed my thumb against a certain spot on Seti's neck, holding it there long enough for her to pass out. It wasn't something I wanted to do, but there was no other option. Seti slumped to the bottom of the boat and Nef gave me a horrified look.

"You killed her," she whispered.

"She is just asleep. Give me the oars."

I snatched them from her and started rowing. The lamps were coming closer. There were three lights and their bearers had split up, likely searching for us. One was close enough to see us any moment. I rowed, choosing speed over silence. Once we were out in the middle of the river, they wouldn't be able to get to us. It was too far to swim, even if one was foolish enough to brave the water in the dark, and by the time they brought a boat, we would be far away.

"Nef, get the sail up," I said. She was still staring in horror at her sister. "Nef."

She seemed to shake herself and finally looked at me.

"Are you sure she is not dead?" she asked.

"Absolutely. I just needed her to be quiet for a while. Now, quickly, the sail. They will see us any moment."

Even as I spoke, someone cried out. We caught the breeze and shot off.

Seti stirred a few moments later and Nef helped her sit up. Seti seemed a little dazed as she looked around. I knew the moment she remembered what had happened because she gave me a fierce glare.

"I said I wanted to go home," she said.

"Be quiet," I said. "Our priority right now needs to be on getting away from here. If you cannot be quiet, I will knock you out again."

She glowered, but Nef whispered to her and Seti turned her back on me. We sailed in silence as the moon rose. It was only a half moon tonight, enough to shed a little light to see by, but hopefully not enough for anyone we might sail past to see us clearly. Tomorrow, perhaps, more men would be searching for us, but I intended to be far away from here by then.

TWENTY-ONE

SETI

I felt funny when I woke up and I didn't realise it was because Tey made me go to sleep until Nef told me. She thought I was dead at first. When I found out, I got so mad at Tey that I couldn't even look at her. I would have jumped right out of the boat if Nef hadn't held my hand and convinced me to stay.

I hated Tey. She was mean and she smelled bad, particularly tonight. She smelled of sweat and dirt and unwashed clothes. I hated this stinking boat and not having a soft bed. I wanted a bath and a hot dinner and my father. I was mad at Nef for not running away with me, even though I asked her to.

We sailed all night. Nef and I took turns to lie down with our head on the other's lap. The boat wasn't big enough for me to stretch out and the wood was too hard, so I didn't sleep much, but my eyes were tired and at least I could rest them. Nef smelled like sweat, although not as bad as Tey did.

"Tey hasn't had any sleep," Nef whispered to me at one point when we were both awake. "And she worked all day, so she is probably really tired. Maybe we should offer to look after the boat so she can sleep for a while?"

"No, let her do it," I said. "It is her job to look after us."

Around midmorning the next day, Tey steered the boat over to the bank. My bladder was almost ready to burst by then and I could hardly hold on long enough to get out of the boat and behind a shrub where Tey couldn't see me. I was in such a hurry that I peed on my foot a bit. I went and stood in the water and made some splashes so I could wash my foot without anyone realising. It meant my skirt got all wet, but today was pretty hot, so I figured it would dry soon.

Tey got out a loaf of bread. She gave Nef and me each a piece and kept a bigger piece for herself. I wanted to throw the bread down in the dirt, but I was really hungry, so I took it but I scowled at her. I wanted her to know I was still mad. I hoped the bread would be stale so I could refuse to eat it, but it tasted fresh. My stomach growled really loudly as soon as the bread was in my mouth. If we had servants with us, they would cook us fresh bread every day and we could eat it while it was still hot enough to burn our tongues.

"Seti, I got you some sandals."

Tey held out a pair of shoes that actually looked new. I wouldn't have worn sandals that had already been on someone else's feet. I was a princess after all, even if Tey seemed to have forgotten.

I glared at her for a little longer before I took the sandals. When I put them on and took a few steps, my feet flopped around in them.

"They are too big," I said.

"They were the smallest ones I could find," Tey said. "Your feet will grow soon enough and it is better to have sandals that are too big than none at all."

"You should have gotten sandals that fit." I pulled them off and tossed them away. "I don't want them."

"Seti, we need to move past these tantrums," Tey said. "Like it or not, this is your life now. The three of us need to be a team, and we cannot do that if you have a tantrum every time you aren't happy about something."

"I told you I want to go home."

"And I have told you a dozen times you cannot. There are bad men waiting there for you. Remember?"

"I have not seen any bad men other than the one you killed. I think you are making it up. Our sister is probably looking for us. She will be mad at you for taking us away."

"Ankhesenpaaten knew she was taking us," Nef said, like she did every time I said I wanted to go home. "Remember, Seti? She came and woke us up and told us to get dressed. Then the captain came and she let him take us. She could have stopped him if she wanted to and he would have had to obey her since she is the queen."

I didn't want to cry in front of Tey, but my stupid eyes filled with tears anyway.

"Ankhesenpaaten doesn't love us," I said. "She wouldn't have let us be taken away if she did."

Nef put her arms around me.

"Maybe," she said. "I don't know."

"Your sister wouldn't have sent you away if she didn't love you," Tey said. "She would have let the bad men do whatever they wanted. But she sent you with me so I could protect you."

She crouched beside me and grabbed my arms to turn me around. Her thumbs dug into the soft spots at the front of my shoulders.

"Seti, I am trying very hard to keep you safe, but I need you to help me," she said. "I cannot protect you if you keep fighting me."

"If you keep causing trouble, she might decide to go away and let the bad men have us," Nef said. "Isn't that right, Tey?"

"I won't do that," Tey said. "I will not let the bad men have you, but it will be much easier for me to protect you if you help me. Can you do that? Your sister wanted you to be safe and you can honour that by helping me."

Nef nodded. I tried to think of a reason to disagree, but I couldn't think of anything, so I nodded too.

"Good," Tey said. "Seti, I need to ask you something. I noticed that when you get upset, it suddenly seems to get windy. Are you doing that?"

I looked away. She knew about the bad thing. I hadn't told her. Had thought she didn't know. I didn't say anything and eventually Tey got up and went to do something with the boat.

TWENTY-TWO
TEY

F or the next week, we sailed through the day and camped on the shore at night. Twice we passed villages that were large enough for me to secure harvesting work. I spent only as much of my barley wages as I needed to and kept the rest. Hopefully, by the time we reached Nubet I would have enough barley saved to secure accommodation, for a while at least.

As I took my last load of lettuce over to the overseer in Iunet, one of the workers fell into step beside me. Like me, he carried a large woven basket filled with lettuce.

"You worked hard today." He gave me an admiring look. "It is rare to see a woman who can keep up such a pace all day while harvesting."

I wasn't the only woman in the fields and I had been too intent on my work to pay much attention to how hard anyone else worked.

"I am used to harvesting," I said.

It wasn't exactly true, but it wasn't as much of a lie as it would have been a week ago. My body was adjusting.

"Are you staying here in Iunet for a while?" he asked. "There will be plenty of harvesting work for a couple of weeks yet."

"No, I am moving on shortly."

We reached the overseer and I placed my basket on the table. The fellow inspected it and gave me a nod, then pointed to where I could collect my wages. I lined up for my bag of barley.

"Can I buy you a drink?"

The man's persistence was making me uneasy, although he had done nothing to warrant such feelings, except he didn't seem to notice my lack of interest. I had done nothing to encourage his attention, but he seemed undefeated.

"I have to get back to my daughters," I said.

"Oh, how old are they?"

Thank Aten he seemed a little less interested now.

"Young enough that I cannot leave them for long."

I received my barley and set off, half expecting him to follow me and surprised when he didn't. I didn't stop for provisions as I had intended. We were running low, but had enough to get by for another day or so. I would rather leave before the man tried to make conversation again.

I watched for him as I headed back to the princesses, not wanting to lead him to them. But he seemed to have lost interest at learning I had young daughters and I didn't see him again.

We passed an amicable night by our campfire. I caught a duck and the princesses were quite proficient at gutting a bird by now, although they were less than thorough when it came to plucking the feathers. They got frustrated and bored with such a lengthy task. I never offered to help them. When they tired of having to pull off the charred and smelly remains of the feathers as they ate, they would learn to do a better job.

I didn't sleep that night, uneasy about the prospect of the man coming looking for me. It was unlikely, but caution was never a bad thing. I sat beside the fire, adding wood from time to time to keep it burning high. Some time after midnight, Nef stirred and sat up.

"Are you not going to bed?" she asked.

"Just keeping watch," I said. "There was a man at the village who was a little too friendly today and I feared he might come looking for me."

"But you need to sleep," she said. "Especially after you worked all day."

"I will be fine. I am trained for this sort of thing. Go back to sleep."

She got up and wrapped her blanket around her shoulders, then came to sit beside me by the fire.

"I can keep watch so you can sleep," she said.

It was the first time either girl had offered to do any more than carry a bundle of supplies and I didn't want to discourage her.

"Fine then. Keep an eye on our surroundings and keep your ears open. If you hear anything that seems out of place, wake me. Listen for things like birds that don't normally sing at night or which sound like they have been startled, branches rustling, frogs that suddenly fall silent."

"I will wake you if anything seems wrong," she said.

I left her to it, although not without misgivings. But it would be a relief if I could trust at least Nef to keep watch for a few hours when necessary. We three would be together for a long time, and I had to trust them at some point. I slept restlessly, regularly jerking awake, but the night seemed calm, nothing was out of place, and Nef was still awake every time I checked. A couple of hours before dawn, I sent her back to bed and resumed my place at the fire. It seemed my uneasiness had been for nothing.

Two days later, we passed the ancient city of Thebes, which was where Pharaoh once ruled from, although other pharaohs had lived in Memphis. It was only Akhenaten, Nef and Seti's father, who had struck out on his own and built a new capital city away from the tradition and history of the old ones. I made the girls huddle down in the boat as we sailed past, although my caution was probably unnecessary. After all, we were a long way from Akhetaten now and Thebes was a big city. It was unlikely anyone would remember us with all the people and boats passing. Still, the prospect of so many people seeing the princesses made me nervous, and I didn't let them get up until Thebes was out of sight behind us.

We sailed for another couple of days and I thought we were only a day or two away from Nubet. We were out of supplies, but I had been reluctant to stop in any of the villages we passed after twice having attracted too much attention. I showed the princesses how to fish and while I hunted, they fished or searched the riverbank for duck eggs and edible tubers. One evening they caught two silvery perch, which they were most proud of.

Our combined efforts had been productive tonight with a fat duck, an eel, and half a dozen eggs. I had even found a handful of sage, which I sprinkled over the duck as it cooked. We were all quite cheery at the prospect of such a fine feast, even Seti who regularly reminded me she didn't like roasted duck. It was too much for us to eat tonight, but I planned to cook the eggs and save them for tomorrow. They would provide a tasty meal as we sailed. My mouth watered and my stomach grumbled at the aroma of the roasting duck and the herbs.

"Tey."

Nef's voice was low and I could barely hear her over the crackle of the fire. She pointed towards the river.

A boat approached, a lamp shining at its bow. No, two boats.

"Get your sandals on." I was already on my feet, a dagger in my hand. "Go hide behind those shrubs. Quickly."

I expected Seti to object, but Nef grabbed her hand and they scurried away. As the boats pulled in to shore, voices reached my ears and I relaxed a little. Two girls bickered. A young woman scolded someone. A man called instructions. They didn't sound like anyone who might be pursuing us. They seemed to take an inordinately long time to secure their boats and unload their belongings. Then they headed straight towards our fire.

"Hello there," a male voice called. "We have left it rather late to stop for the night and we saw your fire. We hoped you wouldn't mind if we joined you."

Two girls around the same age as Nef and Seti raced ahead of the rest of their party.

"They have a duck, Papa," one of them called. "Maybe they won't want to share our fish."

As the adults came close enough to see me, they seemed to hesitate at the sight of my dagger. The man leading them held up his hand.

"Easy," he said. "We are no threat. We are just looking for a place to camp tonight. If you would let us share your fire, we have four perch to share, freshly caught today. We also have bread and some onions."

Others waited behind him, his body shielding them from my view.

"Step out," I called to them. "Let me see how many of you there are."

The man gestured and they came forward. One was around his age, presumably his wife. The two girls might be their daughters. The other woman was older and looked enough like the man to be his mother. Behind them were another couple — a man and woman a few years younger and a child small enough to be carried. This was no more than a family group. I let myself relax and slipped my dagger back into the sheath on my forearm.

"I apologise," I said. "You understand my caution."

"Of course." The man was trying hard to sound cheery, but I caught an edge of unease. He probably wondered whether they had made a mistake in stopping here. "We didn't mean to intrude."

"It is fine," I said. "Girls, you can come out."

Nef and Seti emerged from behind the bushes, their gazes already fastened on the two girls.

"As your daughter pointed out, we have a duck roasting," I said. "There is an eel and some duck eggs as well. We would be happy to share in exchange for a portion of your supplies."

"Excellent." The man sounded more comfortable now.

His family crowded around, laying out blankets and setting the fish on sticks over the fire. Somebody had already gutted them with a neat hand. By the time our duck was ready, the fish were cooked and they had set out their bread and onions on a blanket. We gathered around to eat.

The four girls seemed to strike up an instant friendship and paused their chattering only long enough to gulp down some food. I worried Nef and Seti might say something they shouldn't and tried to keep an ear on their conversation, but from the bits I caught, it seemed innocuous enough. With my belly full, I relaxed.

"So where are you travelling to?" the man, Didia, asked as he licked the last of the duck from his fingers.

"Nubet," I said. "My daughters and I are travelling to my late husband's mother."

"Has it been a long time since you have seen her?" his wife, Beket, asked.

"We have never met her," I said. "My husband moved to Akhetaten in search of work and had not seen his mother for many years. He went to the West a few weeks ago, leaving my daughters and I with nothing. We have no other family, so we travel to his mother in the hope that she will take us in."

"Oh, how terrible," Beket said. "I am so sorry."

"We are travelling to Nubet ourselves," Didia said. "I have lived there all my life, and so has my mother." He gestured towards the old woman, who he had introduced as Khenut. I hadn't heard her speak yet, but she threw me a shy smile. "What is your husband's mother's name? Perhaps my mother or I know her."

"Henuttaneb," I said. "I don't even know whether she is still in Nubet, or indeed whether she lives. My husband had not heard from her for at least a year. But I couldn't think of anywhere else to go."

"Oh, I do indeed know her," Didia exclaimed. "Mother, I am sure you know her too."

Khenut agreed with a nod.

"I do," she whispered. "We played together as girls. She will be so happy to see you, I am sure of it."

"Oh." I didn't quite know how to respond. When I came up

with our cover story, I never anticipated meeting someone who actually knew a Henuttaneb from Nubet. "I am very pleased to hear she lives. That is more than I expected."

"You must travel with us tomorrow," Didia said. "I know where her home is. I can take you straight to her when we reach Nubet."

"Oh, no, we are used to travelling by ourselves," I said. "We would not want to intrude."

"Nonsense," he said. "Henuttaneb would be very cross with me if she heard I left you to make your own way there. Besides, it isn't safe for you to travel alone, just you and the girls. Better that you travel with us the rest of the way and we can see you safely to her."

If I protested too much, he might become suspicious. Surely any woman travelling alone with young daughters would want the security of other companions, especially one that knew the person to whom they supposedly travelled.

"That is very kind of you," I said.

I spent the rest of the evening trying to act normal while I searched for a solution. We would have to go somewhere else — Nubet was no longer a possibility now our cover was ruined. Perhaps one of the princesses could fake being ill? That would give us a reason to stay here when the others moved on in the morning. Then we could head back upriver and go somewhere else.

I waited for a chance to catch Nef's attention — she would be more willing than Seti — but she was too busy playing with the girls, Sitamun and Ipu. I smiled as I watched them chasing each other around. It was good for the princesses to feel normal, even if just for a little while.

TWENTY-THREE

TEY

I tried to get Nef on her own just before she went to sleep, but although I was sure she saw me gesturing at her, she looked away and continued with her game. When it was time for bed, the four girls lay out their blankets next to each other.

"Girls," I called. "Come and say goodnight to your mother before you go to sleep."

They hesitated and I hoped anyone who noticed would assume they were merely reluctant to leave their new friends. They came to me and I wrapped my arms around them.

"We need to get away from these people," I whispered to Nef. "When you wake up in the morning, I need you to pretend to be sick."

She frowned at me.

"I don't want to," she said

"You must. It is not safe for us to travel with them."

She pouted, but one of the other girls ran over to speak to Seti and the moment was lost. They all went back to their blankets and settled down for bed.

"I can take first watch," I said. "Who will take over from me in the middle of the night?"

Didia shot me a puzzled look.

"First watch? Surely you do not sit up all night just in case someone comes by?"

Had I just ruined our cover?

"A woman travelling on her own with two girls?" I said, my voice casual. "One cannot be too careful. Neb usually sits up for a couple of hours so I can sleep. But she can get a full night of rest since there are others here who can help keep watch."

"But what threats do you spot when you sit up all night like that?" Didia asked. "It hardly seems worth it being out in the middle of nowhere as we are."

"I have caught people sneaking around our camp on more than one occasion." I tried not to think about the farmer I killed by mistake. "If you do not have someone keeping watch, you have probably never noticed. Or perhaps we are more of a target since we travel without a man."

Didia looked like he would continue to argue, but his wife leaned over to whisper to him. He sighed.

"Personally, I do not think it necessary, but Beket disagrees," he said. "So I will take the next watch. I assume you will wake me when it is my turn?"

"I will wake you once the moon is right overhead," I said.

They all went off to bed and soon I was the only one awake. The night air was filled with the chirping of insects, the crackle of the fire, and the lingering aroma of fish and roasted duck. Someone snored. A brief gust of wind rustled the tree leaves. Everything was peaceful and I relished the anticipation of getting more than a couple of hours sleep tonight.

I woke Didia when the moon was high. He didn't seem quite awake as he took my place at the fire. As I lay wrapped in my blanket, I watched him for a while, unsure whether he would stay up or if he would simply go back to bed, but once he was properly awake, he seemed content to sit there.

I slept fitfully, waking every few minutes to check Didia was still up. His head lolled at times, but hopefully if anyone was sneaking around, the fact that someone sat up would be enough of a deterrent, even if he dozed.

I must have fallen into a deeper sleep and woke to a riotous chorus of birds. The sun was just peeping over the horizon, accompanied by an orange blaze. Didia still sat by the fire, accompanied now by his youngest daughter. I couldn't remember whether she was Sitamun or Ipu. Nef and Seti were both sound asleep.

"We should be in Nubet by midafternoon," Didia greeted me. "Depending how late this lot sleeps. I suppose there is no hurry, although you must be pleased to be almost at the end of your journey."

"Indeed," I said. "I am very much looking forward to meeting my husband's mother, and I am sure she will be delighted to finally meet her granddaughters."

"Oh, she will be thrilled."

"Do you know her well?"

"My mother knows her better. As she told you, they were children together. I think I remember your husband as well. Menna."

"Yes, Menna," I murmured. Thank Aten Didia had offered a name rather than asking me to confirm it.

"He was a couple of years older than me, so I never had much to do with him," Didia said. "I cannot recall ever speaking with him. He was a woodcarver, was he not? His father had already taught him everything he knew, so he went off to Thebes to learn from a master woodcarver. I thought I heard he went to the West a year or so later, but I must be mistaken."

Had I already told him my "husband" had worked in construction?

"He carved in his younger years," I said. "Not that he spoke of it much. He lost the use of one of his hands in an accident and couldn't carve after that. Perhaps that is what you heard of. You know how such things get twisted. An accident that results in a young man being unable to use his hand, easily becomes news of his death."

"Oh, how terrible," Didia said. "I am very sorry to hear that."

He didn't seem suspicious and I released the breath I hadn't realised I was holding. The rest of his family began to wake, and soon Nef stirred. I waited for her to pretend to be ill, but she lay wrapped in her blanket for a while, chatting with the older girl.

Beket and Khenut passed around bread and dates. Nef took a handful of dates and gobbled them down. I tried to catch her eye, but she didn't look at me, too focussed on her meal. The dates were fresh and chewy, and I ate more than I should have while I waited for Nef. I couldn't tell whether she was avoiding me or just distracted. She seemed to have forgotten she was supposed to pretend to be ill. It wasn't too late, though. As long as we put the plan into motion before we got into the boats, I could still delay our travel. As we packed up our things, I finally got close enough to whisper into Nef's ear.

"Don't forget our plan," I said.

She gave me a blank look.

"You are supposed to be ill, remember?"

She shook her head.

"I don't want to," she said. "I like Sitamun and Ipu. I want to go in their boat today."

"You cannot. We have to get away from these people. It is not safe for us to travel with them."

"Seti won't be happy about that."

Her voice held an ominous tone, and I gave her a sharp look.

"What is that supposed to mean?" I asked.

She shrugged. "She wants to stay with them too and you know what happens when she gets mad."

"What happens?" I asked.

She shook her head and ran back to the other girls. If Nef wouldn't cooperate, we would have to travel with Didia and his family until we reached Nubet. As we sailed, I racked my brain for a way to get away.

Perhaps I could pretend to fall ill myself? But that might only make Didia even more determined to escort us straight to Henut-taneb. If he thought I was ill enough to be unable to care for the girls, he would want to see us safely to their grandmother. We reached Nubet before I could come up with another plan. It was a large and ancient town filled with enormous stone monuments.

We secured the boats and carried our belongings up from the boat.

"Is that all you brought with you?" Didia asked, eyeing our small bundles.

I was suddenly painfully aware he would expect us to have brought what we could carry from our home. Changes of clothing, blankets, mugs, cooking pots. Anything small and light enough to transport.

"I sold everything we owned to buy the boat," I said. "We kept nothing but the clothes we wore and a little food."

"Oh, how sad," Beket said. "Don't you worry. Folk around here are very friendly. Once word gets out that you arrived with nothing, they will help you."

"We really don't need anything," I said. "We can look after ourselves."

"Nonsense," Didia said. "There will be many here who remember Menna. They will want to help his widow. Now, come. Let's not leave Henuttaneb waiting any longer. I will take you to her now. She lives on the other side of town, so it is a bit of a walk."

"Perhaps you could just give me directions," I said. "I wouldn't want to impose any further on your kindness and I would like to pick up some supplies to take with us. So if you tell us where to find her home, we will make our own way there."

"No, no, I will see you right to her door. Don't you worry about supplies. She will not care if you arrive empty-handed."

The rest of his family were going straight home. The girls farewelled each other with many promises to see each other soon. There were even a few tears shed, despite the fact they had met only yesterday. Once his family left, Didia shepherded us through the town, pointing out various sites as we passed. I caught Nef's eye once or twice, trying to remind her she was supposed to fall ill, but she only looked at me blankly.

"You do not need to take us all the way," I said. "You must be eager to go home and relax after your long journey."

"You are very polite," Didia said. "And I understand you feel you are imposing, but please don't worry about it. I would never forgive myself if I didn't escort you all the way and then I later heard you never arrived. How would I ever explain to Henuttaneb?"

Which was exactly what I had been planning. I was starting to feel desperate, but short of knocking Didia out, I couldn't think of any way we could get away from him.

TWENTY-FOUR

TEY

Didia stopped in front of a small cottage which looked like it had been built soundly enough but now desperately needed maintenance. The roof clearly leaked and areas of the mud brick walls had deteriorated. The front yard was mostly sand with a few scraggly weeds and an overgrown patch that might once have been a vegetable garden.

"Henuttaneb," Didia called. "Are you home?"

I held my breath. If we were lucky, Henuttaneb would be out and Didia could leave us here, secure in the knowledge that he had taken us all the way to her home. But the front door opened and an old woman appeared.

Her back was stooped and her face wrinkled. Her head was entirely bald and she wore no wig to cover her scalp. She peered short-sightedly at us.

"Who is it?" she asked.

"It is Didia," he said. "I am Khenut's son."

"Oh, yes," she said. "What do you want?"

"I have with me your son's wife and daughters. My family and I came across them as we travelled back from Behdet. I took it on myself to ensure they reached you safely."

The woman came out of her house to inspect us. She looked at me carefully, then at each of the princesses. I held my breath, waiting for her to tell Didia her son had no wife or daughters.

"Well, then," she said at last. "Come in, my dears. Let's get you settled inside."

"I thought I heard Menna went to the West shortly after he left Nubet," Didia said. "I am so pleased to learn this was not true."

"Yes, yes," she said. "Go on now. You have delivered them safely."

Didia continued talking, but Henuttaneb shooed him away and hurried us inside. She closed the door and looked us over again.

"Well, then," she said. "I assume my son has indeed gone to the West if his wife and daughters have arrived on my doorstep without him."

"Just recently," I said, rather bewildered. Was it really possible Didia had heard the wrong story and Henuttaneb thought her son was still alive until just now? "A construction accident. I am so sorry to bring sad tidings."

"Construction, eh?" she muttered. "So he gave up on the wood-carving, did he?"

She didn't wait for a response, but went over to the shelves and retrieved some mugs.

"Sit down," she said. "You must be parched. I will get you some beer."

The princesses stood close together, looking at me with wide eyes.

"Mind your grandmother," I said to them. "Go sit down."

We sat on a rug which looked like it might never have been washed. While we waited for Henuttaneb, I examined the cottage. Inside was as sorry as the outside and it was dirty as well. If her eyesight was as poor as it seemed, perhaps she couldn't see the state of her home. Henuttaneb shuffled over with mugs for each of us.

"Remember your manners," I said to the princesses.

They probably hadn't been taught much in the way of thanking people. I should have talked to them about such things while we travelled. But if I had expected them to blow our cover, they didn't. They both offered quiet thank yous and Seti even added a cheery *grandmother* to hers.

Henuttaneb awkwardly lowered herself to a cushion, and the four of us stared at each other. I fiddled with my wooden mug, which was smooth under my fingertips and far finer than I had expected. Perhaps it was made by her husband or her son. This might well be a treasured item.

"I am dreadfully sorry to impose on you," I said at last. "I didn't know what else to do. I can see you don't have a lot of room. We will finish our drinks and leave you in peace."

"Of course not," Henuttaneb said. "I would not dream of turning you out. As you say, there is not much room, but we will manage. The girls are small enough to not need much space anyway."

Of any response I might have expected from her, this wasn't it. But if she hadn't seen her son for many years, I supposed she had little reason not to believe. Perhaps it didn't seem unreasonable that her son's widow and daughters would come to find her. Given her obvious poverty, she must wonder why he hadn't thought to see if she needed anything in recent years. A woodcarver would likely lead a modest lifestyle, unless he was an esteemed expert, but surely he would be richer than this. Perhaps it had been many years since her husband went to the West and whatever he had left her was gone.

"I would like to hear about my granddaughters," Henuttaneb said before I could figure out a way to explain any of the things I imagined she must be thinking. "Tell me about yourselves. What are your names? How old are you? Do you have any schooling?"

They answered Henuttaneb's questions, although not without many glances towards me as if to check they were giving appropriate replies. Since I hadn't expected to actually find someone called Henuttaneb who thought she really was their grandmother, I hadn't prepared them with answers for questions about their life. They spoke carefully and made no mention of palaces or servants or private tutors. When at last they had satisfied Henuttaneb's questions, she turned her attention to me.

"Well, then," she said. "I suppose it is your turn. Tell me about my daughter-in-law."

I spoke briefly of my family — this at least was something I didn't need to lie about — and made only the vaguest references to her son, Menna. I didn't know how long ago he had left Nubet and that was a detail she would know. Any other discrepancies could be passed off by saying he had changed after the accident in which he lost the use of his hand, but I couldn't change the date he left.

"You must stay with me, of course," Henuttaneb said.

She struggled to get to her feet and I rose to help her. She thanked me with a pat on my cheek.

"Do you have any way of making an income, dear?" she asked. "Sewing perhaps? I am most happy to have you here, but I have little enough to survive on. I cannot feed an extra three mouths without some help."

"We won't stay long, just a day or two," I said. "I will find us our own accommodation as soon as possible. I am not much of a sewer, but I am used to labouring. I don't expect to have difficulty finding work, especially during the harvest season."

"Labour, eh?" She shot me a shrewd look that made me wonder how much she had gleaned from what I didn't say. "Well, there will be plenty of farmers who won't turn down an extra pair of hands in the fields if you can manage that sort of work."

"I have done it before," I said.

"But as to getting your own accommodation, I won't hear of it. My son would expect his old mother to take in his family. It is right and proper. Now, I think it is about time we started preparing a meal. Why don't you help me, dear? Perhaps the girls might like to explore outside for a while?"

As she took a few vegetables from a basket, I noticed a shelf that hung crookedly.

"If you have a hammer, I can fix this for you." I gave the shelf a wiggle to determine where the problem was.

"Oh, that would be very kind of you. Have a look over there."

She pointed and I quickly found the hammer. It only took a minute to set the shelf right and then I found a cloth and wiped it clean of dust. It obviously hadn't been used in some time. Henuttaneb gave me a puzzled look.

"However did you learn such a thing?" she asked. "Did my son teach you that?"

"I suppose he might have," I said. "I don't really remember. I have always been good at fixing things. I noticed your roof needs patching. I can do that tomorrow for you. And there are some mud bricks that need repairing."

"It has been a long time since I have had any help around the house."

Henuttaneb sliced a cucumber and I noted the awkward way she held the knife. She had bad hands, it seemed. I would do what I could to fix up her home before we moved on. It was the least I could do for her kindness in taking us in.

I felt a pang of guilt every time I looked at her. How must it feel to have her son's wife and children arrive on her doorstep with news of his death? And yet she had been nothing but gracious and kind. We would move on as soon as possible, but perhaps we could stay for a day or two while I figured out where to go. She seemed happy to have us and I could use the time to fix up her house. That at least would make me feel a little less guilty when I disappeared with her "granddaughters".

The next day, I set to work on fixing Henuttaneb's roof. It was in worse condition than I expected and the job took me most of the day. Henuttaneb came out a couple of times to inspect my progress and bring me a mug of beer. She made admiring noises at my work, although I doubted she could see what I was doing, and told me repeatedly how grateful she was. I appreciated the drinks and her visits, as it gave me an excuse to stop for a few minutes. We were well into *shemu* — the harvest season — by now and the day was hot. By the time I had finished, it was too late to find somewhere for us to go today and I wanted to repair the mud bricks tomorrow anyway.

Once I had mended her walls, I tackled the garden. There was indeed an area that seemed to have once been a vegetable patch, although it now contained nothing more than a few onions. It took me a full morning to clear it of weeds, then I dug out another few cubits to make it a little bigger. If she could grow more vegetables, she could perhaps trade the surplus for someone to maintain the garden for her after we were gone.

One of her neighbours spared me some scraps of wood and I built two stools so Henuttaneb wouldn't have to struggle to get up and down from the floor quite so much. She was thrilled and immediately sat on one, gesturing for me to sit on the other. We sat and stared at each other.

"I will start looking for some accommodation of our own tomorrow," I said. "We cannot impose on you any longer."

"Nonsense, dear," Henuttaneb said. "I am enjoying the company and it is so nice to have the young ones around. It has been a very long time since this house has had children in it. Besides, I want to get to know my granddaughters. I have already missed out on so much of their lives. You cannot take them away from me now."

"Perhaps we could stay another day or two."

With each day we stayed, my guilt grew stronger. The more attached she got to the girls, the harder it would be to take them away from her. They were getting attached to her, too. They didn't even hesitate when they called her grandmother. I wanted to remind them she wasn't really their grandmother, that it was all a cover story, but if they started acting differently, Henuttaneb might grow suspicious. I didn't want her to ask questions I couldn't answer, things like when did I meet her son and what kind of woodcarving did he specialise in. There were plenty of questions I wouldn't know the answer to if she thought to ask.

But if Henuttaneb noticed any holes in my story, she didn't mention it. Instead, she suggested I call her Mother. I stumbled over a response, trying to explain that my own mother went to the West when I was very young. She merely patted my hand and suggested I call her Hennie instead.

"I will go out tomorrow and find some work," I said. "If there are other things you need done around the house, I will still be able to do them in the evenings."

"By the gods, you have been good to me." Hennie leaned over to squeeze my hand. "I cannot tell you how grateful I am that you have fixed the roof and the walls and the vegetable garden, and built these wonderful stools. I am so proud my son chose such a useful woman."

As I lay on my mat that night, listening to the soft noises of Hennie and the girls sleeping, I worried about how to get us out of this situation. It wasn't possible to walk away. I had tried so many times to tell Hennie we should leave and she wouldn't even discuss it. So I would have to do it secretly.

If I could get the princesses out of the house with me, we could slip away. I wouldn't be able to tell them we weren't going back until after we left. They wouldn't leave quietly if they knew. I might perhaps say we were going to visit with Sitamun and Ipu. Nef had asked several times when they could see the girls again, but I kept putting her off.

We needed to get back to the wharf, where hopefully our stolen boat would still be, and get out of Nubet. Perhaps we would continue on downriver. We could keep going until we reached Nubia. I would come up with a new cover story on the way. It wasn't a great plan, but it was enough to start with.

But first I would work for a couple of days. I would keep some of my wages for us and leave the rest for Hennie. She had barely enough to survive on — it was clear her husband had left no fortune when he went to the West — but with some extra barley and her newly dug vegetable garden, things would be easier for her. It was the least I could do for her kindness.

The next morning, I left the princesses with Hennie, although not without misgivings. I hoped they wouldn't slip up and say the wrong thing while I was away. It didn't take long to find a farmer who needed help with his harvest. He looked me up and down and seemed doubtful I could do the job, but after watching me work for a few minutes, he was clearly satisfied. At the end of the day, he handed me a bag of barley and told me to come back tomorrow if I wanted more work.

TWENTY-FIVE

SETI

"Well, my dears," Grandmother said after Tey left. "What would you like to do today? We need to clean up the dishes and sweep the floor. Then we should check that lovely garden your mother has been digging and fetch some water for it. It wouldn't do to let it dry out after she has worked so hard. But then we can do something fun. You tell me what you would like to do, hmm?"

She got to her feet awkwardly. She said her knees hurt sometimes and it was hard to get up. I wondered whether my knees would hurt when I got old like her. Nef took her plate and Grandmother's over to the workbench.

"I don't feel very well," I said, not liking Grandmother's long list of chores. I wasn't supposed to say things like how we used to have servants to do all the chores, but it was hard not to. Sometimes the words welled up in my throat and I had to clamp my lips closed to stop them from coming out. It was easier to pretend I was sick and then Grandmother would fuss over me and surely she wouldn't make me do any chores.

Indeed, Grandmother came over and press her hand against my forehead. Her skin was cool, although her hand felt rough.

"Hmm, you don't feel hot," she said. "Where do you feel unwell?"

"In my tummy."

I wrapped my arms around my middle and made a show of bending over and groaning. Grandmother didn't look as concerned as I expected. Maybe she still remembered she wasn't really our grandmother. She was so nice to me and Nef that I thought she had forgotten.

"I know the cure for a sore tummy," Grandmother said cheerily. "Sweeping the floor always makes my tummy feel better. The broom is over there in the corner. Why don't you grab it and start on the floor while Neb and I do the dishes."

I clutched my tummy and groaned again, but Grandmother didn't seem to notice. She was already busy with the dishes and talking to Nef about how many buckets of water we should fetch and that we needed to make sure there was enough left for our mother to bathe when she came home. She didn't seem to know Tey wasn't our mother. I put my hand over my mouth to stop myself from blurting out the truth.

Since Grandmother was still ignoring me, I got up and fetched the broom. I had seen servants sweeping, of course, but I had never paid much attention and didn't quite know what I was supposed to do. I held it in both hands and pushed the broom across the floor.

"Not like that, dear," Grandmother said. She came and took the broom from me. "Hold it like this, see? Have you never swept a floor before?"

She held the broom out to me and I took it back with a shrug.

"No," I said.

"Well, that is strange. How does a girl get to be your age and yet never have helped her mother with the housework? She works so hard, too, your dear mother. You girls are old enough to be more help to her. We shall work on that."

"Our real mother never did any housework," I said as I tried to make the broom do what Grandmother had showed me. It was too big, though, and I was too little.

"Like this, dear." Grandmother put her hands over mine and showed me how to hold the broom again. "Then you move it like this. See how much easier that is?"

I nodded, too intent on the broom to reply. My hands were already sore.

"So who used to do the housework if your mother didn't?" Grandmother asked.

"The servants."

"Oh? And why didn't the servants come with you when you travelled to find me?"

"Because they didn't know we had left."

"Sensen," Nef said. "We are not supposed to talk about that."

"I promise I won't tell anyone your secrets." Grandmother went back to helping Nef clean up the breakfast dishes. "Would you like to tell me more about your life before you came here?"

Nef and I looked at each other. Her mouth was all pinched, as if she was trying not to say things, just like I was. I couldn't hold the words in any more.

"We used to be princesses," I said. "But the bad men want to kill us, so we aren't allowed to talk about it."

"I see," Grandmother said. "So if you were princesses, I suppose you lived in a palace?"

"Uh huh," I said, happy now since she wasn't mad at me for telling her. "We had lots of servants and hot baths every day."

"That sounds wonderful," Grandmother said. "I wish I was a princess, too. Neb, dear, can you get a cloth and wipe down that bench over there? There is still a little water left in the bucket. You can tip the rest on the garden and once Sensen finishes sweeping, we will go to the well."

TWENTY-SIX
TEY

On the way back to Hennie's home, I traded some of my wages for vegetable seeds, which I intended to plant before we left. The girls were sitting in the newly extended garden when I arrived, covered with dirt and busy building a small temple. I crouched down to speak with them.

"How did today go?" I asked. "Did Hennie ask you any questions?"

"Grandmother, you mean?" Seti gave me a wide-eyed stare. "She gave us bread and cucumbers for lunch."

"What sort of things did you talk about?" I asked.

"Nothing much," Nef said.

"I told her about when I was a princess," Seti said, smoothing the dirt that made up one of her temple walls.

Before I could ask what she meant, Hennie called to me from the doorway. She was wearing a wig for the first time since we met her. I supposed that at some point she had decided it wasn't worth wearing anymore and had put it away. I felt a small glimmer of pride that she felt the need to put it back on.

"Tentamun, did you get work?" she asked. "I assume you must have, since you were gone all day."

When I got to my feet, she laughed.

"Oh, I see you did. Come inside. We fetched some water earlier and you look like you could do with a bath."

I waited for her to ask about whatever Seti had said. If I knew exactly what their conversation was, I might be able to explain it away. A child's imaginings, perhaps. A game she used to play with her father. I had a couple of explanations ready, but Hennie didn't mention it. She talked while I washed up, inconsequential news about neighbours I didn't know and various things the girls had done during the day. But she didn't mention Seti saying she was a princess and I couldn't think of a way to ask. As I went to bed that night, it seemed increasingly urgent that we leave this place.

The next morning, I gave Hennie the barley I had earned, as well as the little bag of seeds.

"I will plant those for you tonight," I said. "I meant to do it yesterday."

"Oh, you are so good to me," Hennie said. "I don't know what I have done to deserve such a wonderful daughter-in-law, but I am very grateful. We will have a fine feast waiting for you when you come home tonight. It is time the girls learnt how to cook."

Her words only made me feel more guilty. She thought I acted out of love for her son. She thought the girls and I were going to stay and make a life here with her. I hated knowing I would have to take them away. Better that we leave as soon as possible. All three of them were getting too attached, and the longer I waited, the harder it would be.

I didn't get a chance to speak privately with the girls before I left. I needed to remind them to stick to our cover story, and I still didn't know what Seti told Hennie yesterday. But they lingered in bed and Seti complained about a sore throat. Hennie fussed over them, and nobody seemed to notice when I slipped out the door.

The farmer was happy to see me return and pointed to a row in which to begin work. I ignored everything else around me and focussed on my job. Around midmorning, I felt a tingle up my spine as if someone was watching me. I stood up, resting one hand on my lower back as if it pained me, and looked around.

He stood at the end of a row of cucumbers, staring at me. I let my gaze travel past him, as if paying no attention. If he hadn't realised he was staring, this would make him look away. However, he didn't. I crouched to resume working, but watched him out of the corner of my eye. He made a half-hearted attempt at appearing to work, but even from this distance, I could see he wasn't doing much. The farmer went to speak with him, likely chiding him for not working hard enough. I put my head down and concentrated on the cucumbers.

He seemed to pay me little attention for a while after that, but when I next looked up, he was watching me again. I gave him a hard stare and he still didn't look away. Feeling even more uncomfortable, I turned my back to him. Likely, he was just another lonely man looking to chat with a new worker. By the time we stopped to rest in the middle of the day, he was gone.

When I lined up to collect my barley that afternoon, I overheard the farmer grumbling about someone who had barely done anything but also didn't wait to get paid. It must be the man who was watching me. Was it possible he had been looking for me? Was he staring so hard because he had been trying to figure out whether I was the person he sought? Had somebody seen me leaving with the princesses and passed on my description, perhaps even my identity?

The startled face of the farmer as I pushed my dagger into his belly appeared in my mind. I made assumptions, acted too hastily, and he had paid the cost. I wouldn't make the same mistake again.

I stopped by the market to exchange some of my barley for a few vegetables. A stall displaying clay bowls painted with striking designs caught my eye and I lingered to look. Perhaps I should buy Hennie a gift? She had been far too kind to us and she was minding the girls while I worked. I could say I saw the bowl and thought it was a gift fit for a princess. It might be a good way of introducing the subject of what Seti had told her.

I had been thinking as I worked and figured I could convince her it was just a game the girls played. A story we made up. Something to take their minds off the pain of losing their father and to ease the monotony of days of travel. We had pretended they were princesses, fleeing the palace before Pharaoh's evil advisors could capture them. Maybe I should say something about it, even if Hennie didn't ask. I could casually mention Seti saying she told her about our princess story and ask whether her son had ever created such a story to make his life more exciting.

My hand was on a pretty green bowl when movement at the edge of my gaze made me look up. Nothing seemed out of place, but I took note of my rising unease. Papa taught me to always pay attention when I felt uncomfortable, even if I couldn't see any obvious threat. I left the bowl and walked on. If something happened, I didn't need the distraction of trying not to break a bowl I had spent half my wages on. I purchased some vegetables and set off for Hennie's home.

I was halfway there when the uneasy feeling returned. I stopped and bent over as if scratching my ankle so I could take a quick look behind me. There were few people around here and none seemed to pay any particular attention to me. I couldn't see the man who had been staring at me earlier. I must be imagining things.

But shortly after, my unease returned. I spotted a narrow alley between a bakery and a brewery. With a quick glance around to see if anyone watched, I ducked down the alley, pressed myself against the wall of a building, and waited.

The folk who passed the alley entrance all seemed immersed in their own activities. Two women carrying overflowing baskets of produce chatted about their children. A man who looked like he was on his way home after a hard day of work. A group of children playing some kind of chasing game. One looked down the alley and spotted me. He poked out his tongue and ran off. I waited another few minutes but saw nothing suspicious. I was overre-acting and had let my guilt over the farmer's death get into my head. Despite that, I walked swiftly the rest of the way.

The girls were inside when I arrived. Seti was in a mood and still complained about her sore throat. Nef seemed subdued, although when I asked if she too felt unwell, she shook her head. I placed my hand on her forehead, but she didn't seem to have a fever. I hoped they weren't about to fall ill. Hennie would have immediate reason for suspicion if I didn't know what to do with two sick children.

"I have been keeping an eye on both of them," Hennie said, catching me with my hand to Nef's forehead. "Sensen seems to have grown no worse through the day. Neb doesn't appear to be unwell, although she has been a little quiet."

"Hopefully they will both sleep it off overnight." I set the vegetables on a shelf and handed Hennie the rest of the barley. "I noticed your supplies were running low, so I picked up a few things on my way back."

"Oh, Tentamun, you are too thoughtful," she said. "But you should keep your barley. You already gave me some yesterday and you have worked hard for it. I would have gone out for supplies today, but thought it better for Sensen to rest and I didn't want to leave her alone. "

"I am sure it is nothing," I said. "I will sit with them for a while before bed tonight and we will make up a story to keep them occupied in case she is still unwell tomorrow. While we travelled, we pretended they were princesses. Perhaps we will pretend they are something different this time."

"Yes, Sensen mentioned something about being a princess." Hennie's voice was mild and she didn't show any particular curiosity. She set some of the vegetables aside for tonight's meal and put the rest away in a basket. "It is a good thing to encourage imagination in young children."

"They have very good imaginations. It helped to take their minds off the monotony of our travel, I think. We pretended we were fleeing from Pharaoh's evil advisors."

"Oh, that is a fun story," she said. "I am thinking we will have a cucumber salad tonight. I baked fresh bread this morning. Neb helped me. She said she had never baked bread before, which is unusual for a girl her age."

The princess story didn't seem to have bothered Hennie, but a girl's lack of knowledge about housekeeping could undo us.

"I am afraid I am not much of a baker," I said with what I hoped was an ashamed laugh. "Menna's woodcarving didn't bring in a reliable enough income to raise a family on, so I took work wherever I could. My mother went to the West when I was very young and I never learnt to sew or do other such things that women usually earn an income from. But I have always been fit and strong so I laboured, working in fields or carrying mud bricks at construction sites. I used to pay a woman who lived next door to bake an extra loaf for us each day."

Hennie started chopping the cucumbers.

"I thought you said Menna worked in construction most recently," she said. "I would have thought that would give him a steady income so his wife would not need to work."

"Oh, yes." How much had I said about that? "He went into construction once he couldn't carve anymore."

"Because of the injury to his hand."

"That's right. But before that, his woodcarvings provided an irregular income."

"He was always so talented," she said. "His woodcarvings were in such demand when he lived in Nubet."

"I guess everyone's incomes are tight these days. Folk are just trying to feed their families. Few people have barley left over enough for the prices he demanded. I told him many times he should drop his prices so he could sell more, but he wanted his carvings to be exclusive. He didn't want them to be something anyone could afford. So that left me needing to earn an income if we were to feed the girls."

"Hmm."

Hennie seemed busy with her salad and didn't look at me. Had I said too much? Had something told her the "husband" I spoke of couldn't possibly be her son? My throat was suddenly dry and I swallowed hard.

"I should go check the garden," I said. "Make sure no weeds are growing yet."

"I will call you when dinner is ready," Hennie said. "It won't be long."

I fled the house, eager to get away before I said anything else to make her suspicious. We couldn't stay here much longer. If Hennie hadn't already noticed the holes in my story, she would soon enough. The more I said, the more likely she was to realise it was all a lie.

TWENTY-SEVEN

TEY

As we prepared for bed that evening, I checked the door was locked and the windows secured. One shutter was a little loose, and I worried it might be too easy for someone to knock it out. It only took me a couple of minutes to fix it, then I checked the door again.

I retrieved my daggers from their various sheaths and lay them out on my bed mat, checking for any signs of rust or damage. One or two needed sharpening, and I made a mental note to do that tomorrow morning before I left for work. When he gave me my first dagger, Papa told me I would never regret sharpening it as soon as it needed it. I didn't realise Hennie was watching until she spoke.

"I wonder about what sort of mess my son left behind that a woman would feel the need to carry so many weapons," she said.

Her voice held no judgement and gave me little idea of what she thought.

"A woman who does the sort of work I do often finds herself the target of unwanted attention," I said. "When your husband is not with you because he is busy with his own work, a woman needs to be able to defend herself."

"But surely a single weapon would be sufficient," she said.

I studied the dagger in my hand, trying to find a response.

"Be at ease, Ten," she said. "I am not asking you to share whatever part of your story you are trying to keep to yourself. I was merely observing. From the way you handle those weapons, it is clear you know how to use them, which is unusual for a woman. But you do not need to tell me anything. The secrets you have brought with you are safe in this house."

She put out the lamp and I took that as a sign the conversation was over. As I waited for sleep, I wondered what she meant about the secrets I had brought. Did Hennie suspect more than she let on?

Seti seemed to be back to her usual self the next morning, and I felt a little easier about leaving them. I was reasonably sure that what I told Hennie about the princess story should have calmed any suspicion she had. Although, I realised as I walked to the farm, she would have no reason for suspicion, even if they insisted they were princesses. Who would believe such a thing and from girls of their age? Surely plenty of children went through stages where they imagined themselves to be someone else. My guilt about lying to Hennie had overshadowed the extent of what Seti said. There was nothing to be worried about.

Hennie was more likely to grow suspicious because I said the wrong thing about Menna, although the fact that it had been many years since she had seen him would obscure most errors. I wished I knew exactly how many, though. That was the main thing that might reveal my lie.

I turned my thoughts to the man from yesterday. He had definitely been staring at me in the field, but I wasn't sure whether I imagined someone following me later. If he turned up again today, I would confront him and ask why he had been staring at me. We might only be in Nubet for another couple of days, but I didn't intend to spend that time looking over my shoulder.

But when I reached the field, he wasn't there and although I watched for him through the morning, he never arrived. Good. That was one less thing to worry about. As I waited for my wages that afternoon, two men behind me in the line were engaged in a debate about the best way to catch fish. One of them tapped me on the shoulder and asked, jokingly, if I would intervene and tell them who was correct. I offered my opinion, which was different to either of theirs, and they laughed. My mood was high as I reached the front of the line and accepted my bag of barley.

"My harvest is almost finished," the farmer said. "I only have another day or two of work for you, but I have a friend who still needs help. I have noticed how hard you work and I would be more than happy to recommend you to him once we finish here."

"Thank you," I said. "I would be most appreciative."

I didn't tell him I hoped I wouldn't need any more work. Let him think he was helping me out. I stopped to talk briefly to one of the female workers who caught my eye and gave me a shy smile. I didn't detour via the market today, and although I paid careful attention to the people around me, I saw nothing that made me suspect anyone watched me. My anxiety yesterday was an over-reaction.

When I reached the house, Seti was sitting in the dirt out the front, absorbed in a game involving several small carved figures — something made by Hennie's husband, perhaps? — and a handful of pebbles. I watched for a few moments, but couldn't make much sense of the game. The pebbles seemed to be following the figures, but that was all I could understand. She didn't notice me until I crouched in front of her.

"Are you feeling better today?" I asked, putting my hand to her forehead.

She ducked away and frowned at me.

"I was playing," she said. "And you are messing it up."

She pointed and I realised I had stood on one of her pebbles.

"Oh, sorry," I said. "Where is Nef?"

"She went to get water."

My heart beat a little faster. Calm down, I told myself. Hennie took them to the well every day.

"How long ago?" I asked, careful to keep my tone casual.

Seti shrugged. "I don't know. A while."

I got to my feet and watched her for another few moments. She was already immersed in her game again and seemed to have forgotten I was there. I went into the house. The lingering aroma of fresh bread made my stomach stir.

"Hello, Tentamun," Hennie greeted me. "How was work?"

"Hot," I said. "We are almost finished, but the farmer says he will recommend me to a friend. I should be able to get more work easily enough."

"That is good." She sounded a little absent as she searched for something on a shelf.

"Sensen says Neb went for water," I said. "Has she been gone for long?"

"Oh, there it is. Neb? She should have been back by now. She probably isn't far away."

Calm, I told myself. Breathe in and out before you speak.

"I might go meet her," I said. "I am a little concerned in case she is coming down with whatever Sensen had yesterday. She shouldn't exert herself too much."

"I have kept a close eye on both of them," Hennie said. "No sign of fever and Neb hasn't complained about a sore throat at all."

"Still, I will go meet her. Where is the well?"

Hennie gave directions, and I set off. As I passed Seti, I hesitated. I almost didn't say anything, convinced I was overreacting.

"Seti, maybe you should go inside?" I said. "You weren't well yesterday. Perhaps a rest would do you good."

"I am playing," she said.

"Go inside, Seti."

"I don't want to."

A gust of wind swirled the sand in Hennie's front yard. I watched it for a moment, more convinced than ever this was Seti's doing. I could stay and argue with her, and she would sulk all night, or I could go find Nef and bring her back. Seti would likely be happy enough to come inside once her sister was home.

"I am going to help Nef bring the water," I said.

Absorbed in her game, Seti didn't respond.

I watched for Nef on my way to the well. Perhaps she had started to feel unwell after all and found the bucket too heavy. She might have found a shady spot to sit and rest. But I didn't see her anywhere and there was no sign of her at the well. I asked a pair of women who chatted nearby whether they had seen a girl come to fetch water.

"Nobody has come while we have been here," one of them said.

I made myself exhale a long, calming breath as I searched around the well. There was nothing that might have grabbed Nef's attention and distracted her from her task. I called her, in case she had gone to sit somewhere nearby, but there was no reply. At last I started back towards Hennie's home. She must have stopped somewhere along the way and I had missed her.

I encountered a group of children playing a skipping game on a side road. When I asked if they had seen Nef, they all shrugged and shook their heads. She was probably back at Hennie's by now.

I wanted to run back as fast as I could, but I made myself walk, albeit at a brisk pace. If Nef was sitting somewhere off the path, I didn't want to miss her and then worry when she wasn't back at the house. I was halfway there when I spotted an overturned bucket in a side street. It was dry inside. If this was the bucket Nef took with her, she never made it to the well.

I was still telling myself I was overreacting, even as I ran back to Hennie's home. Seti was still playing out the front. I rushed straight past her and burst into the house.

"Nef?" I called. "Nef, are you here?"

Hennie came in from the other chamber.

"Tentamun, whatever is the matter?"

"Did Nef come back?"

She stared at me blankly and I realised I had used the wrong name.

"Neb, I mean. Sorry, I am just so worried."

"No, she hasn't returned," Hennie said slowly. "I thought you went to meet her."

I showed her the bucket.

"Is this yours?" I asked.

She took it from me and turned it over, then pointed to a mark on the base.

"Yes, this is mine," she said. "That mark tells me my husband made it. Where did you find it? I thought Neb would have taken it with her."

"It was lying in an alley halfway to the well."

Hennie gave me a confused look.

"But where is Neb?"

"I don't know," I said. "I fear she has been taken."

"Taken? By who?"

I shook my head and headed back outside. Hennie followed close behind me.

"Sensen, I need you to come into the house right now," I said.

Seti set down the little wooden figures.

"Where is Nef?" she asked.

There was no point in correcting her since Hennie had already heard me use that name as well.

"I don't know," I said. "That is why I need you to come inside."

"Where is my sister?" Tears trembled and she clenched her fists. "I want to see Nef."

"Sensen, come inside. I am going to find Neb, but I need you to come in first."

"Where is Nef?" she shouted as she got to her feet. She put her hands on her hips and glared up at me.

"Sensen, please listen to me. I don't know where she is and I don't have time to argue with you. I need to go find her, but I want you to go into the house first so I know you are safe. Stay inside with Hennie."

"Did the bad men come and take her?" Seti's voice was very quiet now.

"Maybe. I don't know yet."

"Did they hurt her?"

Sand swirled around us.

"Sensen, you need to stop that."

"Tell me where Nef is."

The wind blew harder. Sand grazed my cheek and I shielded my eyes with my hand.

"Sensen."

Seti glowered at me.

"You lost her," she said. "You are supposed to keep us safe. That is your job."

"Sensen, keep your voice down."

Seti locked eyes with me. The sand circled us and it was like we were in the middle of a storm. So much sand filled the air that I couldn't even see through it anymore. I could see nothing but Seti.

"Make it stop," I said, sharply.

Seti crossed her arms over her chest.

"You let the bad men take Nef," she said.

"I am going to find her just as soon as you go inside."

The sand circled us faster. It tore at my skirt and my hair. Sand nipped my arms. If it knocked me off my feet, I would be sucked up into the tunnel that stretched above us.

"Seti," I yelled. "Stop it right now."

"I cannot," she cried. "I don't know how."

I grabbed her arms.

"Look at me," I said. "Seti, look at me and don't think about anything else. I want you to breathe. Nice, deep breaths. That is good. Keep going. A long breath in and an even longer one out. That is it. Do it again."

The sand slowed.

"Keep breathing," I said. "Come on, another breath in. Keep looking at me."

The sand dropped to the ground.

"That is it, Seti. Good girl."

Seti's face crumpled.

"I didn't mean to do it," she said.

"I know," I said. "It is all right. But I need to go find Nef now. Can you go inside with Hennie? Please?"

Seti nodded, shame-faced now her temper had passed.

I took her hand and turned to find Hennie standing in the doorway, her hand over her mouth. I met her gaze and shook my head.

"Later," I said. "I need to find Neb. You and Sensen should stay inside. Lock the door and don't let anyone in until I get back."

Hennie reached for Seti's hand.

"Come inside, dear," she said. "Bring your little wooden men and we will play a game while your mamma is gone."

TWENTY-EIGHT

SETI

As soon as we got inside, Grandmother closed the door and pulled down the bar to lock it.

"Would you like a drink, dear?" she asked. "You must be thirsty after being outside for so long."

"I want Nef," I said.

"Your mother has gone to find your sister and bring her home. I am sure she is well."

"The bad men have got her."

"Come into the bedchamber and lie down," Grandmother said. "That is it, dear. Just lie on your mat and calm yourself. Now, tell me about the bad men. Who are they?"

"I don't know."

I rolled over onto my side so my back was to her. I didn't want to talk to Grandmother. I wanted to see Nef.

"Why are the bad men looking for you?" Grandmother asked.

"To kill us."

"Why is that, my dear? Does it have something to do with you being a princess?"

"I am not supposed to talk about it." I had said too much again. Tey would be mad at me.

"Your mother is trying to keep both you girls safe." Grandmother's voice was too cheery and I didn't think she understood. "She will find your sister and you will be together again soon enough."

"The bad men have probably already killed her."

"Your mother is a very capable woman, Sensen. She will find your sister. We just have to be patient and wait for her."

"But she wasn't here." My eyes couldn't hold the tears in any longer and they leaked out. "By the time she finds Nef, it will be too late and she will have gone to the West like our sisters."

"How many sisters do you have?" Grandmother asked.

"Five. But there are only two left."

"And where is your other sister who is still alive?"

"At the palace. She let him take us away and didn't even try to stop him. I think she hates me and Nef."

"Why do you keep calling her Nef, dear?" Grandmother asked.

I had said the wrong thing again.

"I cannot tell you," I said.

I was so miserable about Nef being missing that my stomach hurt. I wrapped my arms around my middle and groaned.

"Does your tummy hurt again?" Grandmother asked. "How about I get you a drink? That will sort you out."

At least she hadn't suggested I sweep the floor to make me feel better. I swallowed and realised my throat was feeling rather dry after all.

"Maybe I could have something to eat as well?" I asked. "I am sure that will make me feel better."

"Of course, my dear. Why don't you come and help me in the other chamber? Your mother and your sister will be very hungry when they get back. We will have a meal ready so they can eat as soon as they are home."

I waited until I heard Hennie lock the door, then ran back to where I found the bucket. I searched the alley, looking for anything that might tell me what direction Nef had been taken. Finding nothing, I expanded my search to the surrounding streets and spotted a sandal. It was the right size, although I wasn't sure it was Nef's. I continued searching the length of that street, then worked my way along each street off it. I found a second sandal, which was a match for the first.

The light was fading and without a lamp, I wouldn't see any more clues. But I could check the windows of the nearby houses. If Nef was here, I would find her. I didn't let myself think about how she might have already been taken away from Nubet.

I started with the house nearest where I found the second sandal, then made my way along the street. If the shutters were open, I looked in windows and I listened at them when they were closed. I heard much about the minutiae of folks' day. Children played, babies cried. A vicious argument between husband and wife, which ended with pottery smashing against a wall. I saw a couple of things I would rather not have, but those people were not my responsibility.

I hoped to hear somebody talk about seeing a young girl being carried away, but if anyone spoke of such a thing, it wasn't while I listened at their window. It was close to midnight by now, and if Nef was in one of these houses, she was probably asleep. I wouldn't learn anything else tonight.

I walked back to Hennie's home, dreading the moment I would have to tell Seti I hadn't found her. Perhaps she would be asleep by the time I got back. I knocked on the door.

"Hennie, it is Tentamun," I said softly.

Seti was already asking if I had Nef, even as Hennie unlocked the door. Their faces were pale and the dark circles under Seti's eyes told me she should have been asleep hours ago. I locked the door, then crouched down to Seti's eye level.

"I haven't found her yet," I said. "There is nothing more I can do in the dark, but I will go back out again at dawn. I will find her, I promise."

"You need to get some sleep, my dear." Hennie set her hand on Seti's shoulder. "Sensen, we agreed you would go straight to bed as soon as your mother returned. Off you go now."

I half expected another tantrum, but Seti only wiped her tears and went to the sleeping chamber without complaint. Hennie gave me a steady look.

"We saved you some dinner," she said. "You should eat, then get some rest. Tomorrow will be a big day."

"I suppose I owe you an explanation," I said.

"Not tonight, dear. You have had a long day and a terrible shock. When we have Neb back safe and sound will be soon enough for us to talk."

I ate the meal she had prepared for me, although the bread stuck in my throat, then went to bed. As I lay in the dark, listening to Seti crying, I cursed myself. Why didn't I pay more attention to the man I thought was watching me? No wonder he hadn't come to the field today. He had probably been waiting for a chance to grab Nef.

But why did he take only one girl and not both? Perhaps Nef gave him the perfect opportunity when she went to fetch water alone. It would have been harder to snatch Seti from Hennie's doorstep without the woman hearing. Perhaps he had come here, but Hennie was outside with Seti or watching her from the doorway.

I wondered whether Hennie might have had anything to do with it, but quickly dismissed the idea. She had no reason to think we were anything other than we claimed — her dead son's wife and daughters. If she had grown suspicious, she would have confronted me, then turned us out of the house. She wouldn't let us continue living here if she thought we were anyone other than who we claimed to be. And what woman would take part in abducting a girl she believed to be her granddaughter? She looked as upset as Seti. No, Hennie had nothing to do with it.

It had to be the man in the field. He had followed me back to Hennie's home yesterday, or an associate of his had. Perhaps there had been more than one man watching me.

I had made such a mess of things. I was only relieved Papa wasn't here to see it. Or Intef. We might not have always gotten along, but Intef thought so highly of my skills that he had entrusted his beloved queen's sisters to me. What would he think if he knew I had lost one of them before the turning of the first season?

I tossed and turned and barely slept. Once or twice I dozed off, but I dreamed someone snuck into the house while we slept and snatched Seti as well. I woke, my heart pounding, and crawled over to her mat. She lay sprawled with her arms outstretched and her blanket only half over her. Her cheeks were still shiny with tears. I pulled up her blanket, then went to check the door was still locked. I checked each of the windows but felt too uneasy to lie down again, so I prowled around the other chamber.

"Cannot sleep?" Hennie appeared in the doorway of the sleeping chamber.

"I am sorry. I didn't mean to wake you."

"I wasn't sleeping much anyway. Too worried about Neb."

"I dreamed someone came into the house and took Sensen. I cannot go back to sleep after that."

"I dreamed someone came and took both of you." Hennie shot me a wry look. "Strange that your vast number of daggers didn't seem to be in my dream. I doubt someone would get their hands on you without getting a dagger in them."

I winced, thinking of the farmer I had killed.

"Tell me, dear, what kind of trouble are you in?" Hennie asked. "There might be more I could do to help you if I knew the whole story."

I sighed heavily and lowered myself to the rug. It wasn't fair to keep letting her think it was her granddaughter who had been abducted, but the more she knew, the more danger she would be in. Or was it too late? Would anyone who knew our true identities assume Hennie knew too?

Hennie sat opposite me and leaned over to squeeze my hand.

"It cannot be that bad, but it is time for the truth," she said.

I raised my gaze to meet hers. There was no judgement in her face, only kindness and compassion.

"You know, don't you?" I asked. "I am not your son's wife. I never knew him. I am so sorry."

"I know," she said. "Menna went to the West more than ten years ago. Too long for you to be old enough to have married him or for those to be his daughters. If he had a wife he never wrote to me about, it wasn't you."

"Why didn't you say something? Why did you take us in and pretend you believed us?"

"You needed help. I couldn't imagine what trouble you might be in that you would find an old woman and pretend to be her dead son's wife, but I assumed it must be dire. I knew you would tell me when the time was right. The girls, however, have let slip a little more of their story than you might have intended."

"Seti told you they were princesses."

Seti's name slipped out of my mouth, but it was too late to take it back.

"She did indeed. I might have thought nothing of it if I didn't already know you weren't who you said you were. So tell me, who are they? And who are you to them? I assume you are not really their mother."

"What gave me away?" I asked, a little bitterly.

Hennie smiled and patted my hand.

"You don't have the motherly instinct," she said. "You say the right things, but the look in your eyes when you see them and the way you touch them, those things tell me you are not their mother."

She waited in silence while I tried to find the right words.

"Seti told the truth when she said they were princesses," I said. "I don't know whether the news has reached as far as Nubet yet, but Pharaoh Akhenaten went to the West a few weeks ago. His heir has taken his place on the throne, although his first wife has also gone to the West. On the throne beside Pharaoh now sits the princess Ankhesenpaaten, third daughter of Akhenaten. The girls are her younger sisters, Neferneferuaten Tasherit and Setenpenre. They prefer to be called Nef and Seti. Should something happen to their sister, those girls are the last remaining daughters of their mother's bloodline. Nef, and then Seti, would be queen next."

"And I assume that causes a problem?"

Hennie didn't seem at all surprised to learn the two girls who had been pretending to be her granddaughters were the queen's sisters.

"Pharaoh's chief advisors wanted them out of the way," I said. "As long as there are three daughters of Akhenaten alive, two of them are disposable. The queen was told they would need to be killed so they couldn't be used against her. She chose instead to send them away."

"And how did you come to have the task of shepherding away two princesses before they could be killed?"

"My brother is captain of the queen's personal squad. She

entrusted the matter of sending them away to him. I offered to take them."

"But why?" Hennie asked. "I might understand if they were relatives of some kind, but it seems they were strangers to you, yes?"

"I had never met them before the moment my brother handed them over to me and we fled the palace. As to why, I wanted to control my own life. I wanted to do something important, something more than breeding babies and keeping some man's house. My father is a foot soldier and he has trained me ever since I was old enough to understand what that meant."

The only sign of Hennie's surprise was a slight rising of her eyebrows.

"And as a woman, you could not be a soldier yourself," she said.

"No, I could never be a soldier. But I can be a guardian to those girls. Hennie, I am so sorry. I never intended to mislead you. When we ran into Didia and I told him our cover story, I never imagined he would know somebody with the name I gave him. He insisted on escorting us to you, and I couldn't get away without making him suspicious. Then when you pretended you believed us, I guess it was just easier to go along with it for a couple of days. I meant to move on soon. I was only intending to fix up your house for you, to thank you for your kindness, and then we were going to leave. But every time I tried to go, you convinced me to stay a little longer."

"Where would you have gone? Here, the girls have a home. Stability. After being on my own for so many years, I have welcomed the sound of children in the house. It is not something I ever thought to have again."

"We stayed too long, though," I said. "Someone found us. I thought a man was watching me yesterday, following me perhaps, but I told myself I was overreacting. On our way to Nubet..." My voice trailed away. I wasn't yet ready to confess my mistake. "There was an incident and I reacted too quickly. I have tried to learn from that and to be more cautious. But my caution might have cost Nef her life."

"Do you really think they have killed her?"

"I don't know. If the intention was to dispose of the princesses, I would expect them to take Seti as well and kill them both. That they took only the eldest makes me suspect this is not about eliminating the competition. I think they will take her back to Akhetaten to make her queen."

"But what use is such a young queen?"

"I suppose that is the point. Once Nef returns, their sister, the queen, will disappear. Then Pharaoh will have a nasty accident and if he hasn't yet named his own heir, the chief advisors will have to select one. They might choose one of their own men, someone who will do whatever they want. But the girls also have a younger brother. With a child pharaoh on the throne, and a child queen who is too young to act as regent, somebody else will have to take charge. By the time Pharaoh and his queen are old enough to understand, it will be too late."

"And what would happen to their older sister? The one who is already queen?"

"They will kill her. There can only be one queen, and as long as she lives, she might find a way to reclaim her throne."

And my brother would help her if he lived through that. If she was deposed, he would do anything he could to help her get her throne back.

"Would she kill Nef to do so?" Hennie asked.

"I don't think so. If she had any inclination to kill her sisters, it would have been easier to do it than to send them away and risk them returning or being found. But that doesn't mean others won't act on her behalf and without her knowledge."

"Why did she not send more guards with her sisters? Surely the protection of two princesses who are in direct line for the throne would warrant at least a full squad of trained men."

"They had to slip away quietly and trained soldiers are unmistakable to anyone who knows what to look for. There is no way they could pass as anything but what they are. With just one guard, they could disappear. And with their guard being a woman, nobody would look at us twice, even though I am probably as well trained as any soldier. Or at least, that was the plan."

"I saw something earlier." Hennie's voice was hesitant now. "When you told Seti to come inside, a storm suddenly rose up. I cannot see much unless it is right in front of my face, but I saw enough to know it was a storm that came out of a clear sky and seemed to affect nothing but my own garden."

I gave a heavy sigh and studied my hands.

"I don't know what to tell you," I said. "I think it is Seti's doing. It happens sometimes when she gets upset. I don't know whether she quite realises she is doing it and I don't think she can control it."

"Dear Aten," Hennie said. "Such a great responsibility for one so young."

I wasn't sure whether she meant me or Seti.

"So what will you do now?" she asked.

"As soon as the sun rises, I will go out again and search for Nef. I think the man who was watching me will have some answers. If he doesn't have Nef, he knows who took her."

"And how will you get those answers out of him, assuming you can find him?"

I gave her a steady look.

"Don't ask me that," I said. "It is not something you need to know."

"While you look for Nef, I will keep Seti safe," Hennie said. "We will lock the door and stay inside. If anyone comes looking for her, they will have to break down the door."

"If someone comes for her, they won't hesitate to break through the door or the walls or whatever they must. They won't leave you alive either if you get in their way. Are you sure you don't want me to take her with me?"

"You cannot do what you must with a child slowing you

down," she said. "Leave her here with me so you can focus on finding Nef."

"Thank you, Hennie. For your kindness."

"I am only glad you have told me the truth, my dear. But tell me, you have given the girls' real names, but what is yours? It does not seem right that I keep calling you Tentamun."

"Tey," I said. "My name is Tey."

THIRTY

TEY

A s soon as dawn broke, I left Hennie's house and made my way through the city. The streets were still quiet. Lamplight flickered behind shuttered windows. Smoke and the aroma of freshly baked bread drifted on the breeze. A donkey brayed and a baby cried. I had always liked early morning, when dawn was new and the day still full of possibility.

The farmer was already out in his field, although none of the other workers had arrived yet.

"Tentamun," he called. "You are early today."

"I am afraid I am not here to work," I said. "I am looking for someone. There was a man here two days ago. He was picking cucumbers, but he disappeared partway through the day. I heard you saying afterwards he hadn't come to collect his pay."

"Oh, yes, I know who you mean. I had never seen him before, but he came looking for work and I never turn away an extra pair of hands during harvest. He hardly did anything, though, and he left before noon."

"Who is he?"

"I don't think he gave his name."

"Did that not seem odd to you?"

He shrugged.

"Not particularly," he said. "As long as a person looks like they can cope with the work, I don't care who they are."

"Did he say where he was from?"

"No, I am afraid I never spoke to him again after I agreed to let him work for the day, other than around midmorning when I went to tell him he was not working hard enough."

"Did you notice him speak to anyone else while he was here? Is there someone who might know who he is?"

"He didn't talk to anyone as far as I know. He did arrive at the same time as another man, though. I didn't see them talking to each other, but I thought I caught him giving the other fellow a look at one point, as if he conveyed a message of some sort."

"Who was it?"

Other workers had arrived by now. Some were already out in the field, while others stood around chatting.

"Him." The farmer nodded. "The fellow who is off by himself over there. The one watching us."

I went straight over to the man. He didn't look at all bothered when he saw me approaching. When I reached him, I didn't hesitate. I tackled him and sent him flying backwards. Before he could recover, I flipped him onto his belly and held his face in the dirt.

"Where is she?" I asked.

He squawked and I pulled his head up so he could speak.

"I don't know what you are talking about," he spluttered.

"Wrong answer."

I punched his back, right where his kidneys were. He groaned and went still for a moment. Then he fought me, but he was already face-down and it took little effort to keep him there. I rested my dagger against his neck and he stopped moving.

"I do not intend to waste a lot of time trying to convince you to talk," I said. "I am only going to ask you once more. If I don't like the answer you give me, I will slit your throat and be done with you. Do you understand?"

"I don't know anything."

I pressed my dagger into his neck, just enough to draw blood.

"Wrong answer again," I said. "Now where is she?"

I put a little more pressure on the dagger to reinforce how serious I was.

"I don't know what you are talking about and that is the truth," he said. "There was a man asking around a couple of days ago. I guess he is who you are looking for. I didn't do whatever you think I did."

"What was he asking?"

"He was looking for a woman soldier. I thought he was joking. Whoever heard of a woman soldier? It is a ridiculous idea."

How did they know? Was Papa safe? Or had they figured out enough to take him and torture him? He didn't know where I had gone, though. There would have been little he could tell them. I pressed a little harder on the dagger.

"No, no, I will tell you everything," he said. "Please, just let me speak."

I eased off a little.

"He said she kidnapped two girls and their family had paid him to find them. Then you turned up the next day. I didn't know whether you were who he was looking for, but you are obviously fit and strong, so when I ran into him again, I told him I had seen a woman who might match the description he gave. He came to see. I didn't speak to him again and I don't know anything else."

"Where were you when you first met him?"

"Down at the harbour. I get some extra work from time to time unloading boats. He was going around talking to everyone there."

The harbour. Why didn't I think of that? If Nef was alive and he needed to get her back to Akhetaten, he would have to take her on the Great River.

I left him lying face down in the dirt. I took no notice of the men who had gathered nearby to watch, clearly wondering if they should intervene. As I ran off, I heard one of them muttering about me being unnatural. It wasn't the first time a man had called me that and I doubted it would be the last.

THIRTY-ONE

TEY

I had never run so fast in my life. Please let her still be there, I prayed. Please don't let him have taken her away yet.

The wharf was busy with several boats preparing to leave and I couldn't see the man I wanted. I spoke to the captains of each of the departing boats, but none had any passengers travelling with a young girl. I implied I had run from a violent husband who had threatened to kill both me and my daughters and who had now taken one of them. I received mixed responses since most folk believed it was a man's right to discipline his wife and that the children belonged to him anyway.

I stopped everyone I could find and described the man I was looking for. Nobody remembered him, which seemed rather odd. Surely the man I left in the dirt of the farmer's field was not the only person he had approached. I watched folk boarding the boats that were being prepared for departure, but saw no sign of either Nef or the man. When there was nobody left to question, I sat in the shade for a while. My stomach growled and I was light-headed with thirst, but I couldn't leave and risk missing Nef if they brought her to a boat.

It was the middle of the afternoon before I finally found

someone who remembered a man asking about a woman and two missing girls.

"Yes, yes," he said. "I didn't like the look of the fellow. Something seemed off about him. I told him I knew nothing, but I would have said that even if I knew who he was looking for."

"Is there anything else you remember about him?" I asked. "Something that might help me identify him? Did he say where he was staying?"

"No, he said nothing about who he himself was, other than that he was hired to locate these girls. I do remember which boat he arrived on, though. Perhaps you could ask the captain if he knows anything else?"

Relief made my limbs weak. A breakthrough, at last.

"Where is he?" I asked.

"He has only just arrived. That is him over there. I would guess he is not sailing until tomorrow since he has arrived so late in the day."

"Thank you," I said. "You have been an enormous help."

"I hope you find him," he said. "I hope you get whatever satisfaction you are looking for."

I gave him a brief smile and headed over to the captain.

"Yes, I know the fellow you mean," he said. "I came downriver from Thebes. Picked him up about halfway along and dropped him off at the wharf here. He went around asking everyone about these girls he was looking for. He kept to himself other than that. Haven't seen him again since we left him here three days ago. He knows I was heading back upriver again and had expected to be here today or tomorrow, so perhaps he will turn up shortly."

"I will wait and see if he comes then," I said.

I found an unobtrusive place where I could watch his boat. The rest of the afternoon passed with no sign of the man. The day was hot and I sweated even though I did no more than stand in the shade. At length, it became clear the captain was getting ready to leave his boat for the night, so I went to speak with him again.

"I am afraid I haven't seen him," he said, when he saw me

approaching. "I don't know what your story is, but my sister ran away from a husband who would have killed her. She lives with me and my wife now. I am sympathetic to any woman who finds herself in such a situation. Tell me where you are staying and I will send a messenger if I see him. I will hold the boat to give you time to get back, but I cannot stay for long. I have a schedule to keep to."

"I am most appreciative," I said, and told him where to find Hennie's home.

I waited at the wharf a while longer, but by the time the sun set, there seemed little point in lingering. The wharf had cleared, the sailers presumably having gone off to make the most of a night on land and the wharf workers gone home. I dreaded telling Seti I hadn't found Nef yet.

Seti was waiting at the window as I approached the house. Her face fell when she saw me. As I opened the door, the aroma of fresh bread wafted out and my stomach stirred. Hennie must have been baking to distract herself.

"You don't have her," Seti said.

"I am sorry, Seti. I am doing everything I can. I think I know who took her."

"Why did you come back then?" she cried. "Why aren't you out there looking for her?"

"Seti, dear." Hennie appeared behind her in the doorway and placed her hands on Seti's shoulders. "There is not much Tey can do in the dark. Let her come in and sit down. She has been looking for your sister all day, and I am sure she needs to eat and rest."

"I will go out again first thing tomorrow," I said. "I will find her, Seti. I promise."

Seti glowered, but Hennie steered her away from the doorway.

"There is no water for washing, I am afraid," Hennie said. "I could have gone and taken Seti with me, but I feared she might be snatched if we left the house."

"I will go," I said. "Let me just have something to drink first."

Hennie brought me a mug of beer and I drained it in moments. My parched throat felt little better, but at least my mouth was wet. I didn't feel like walking all the way to the well, but it meant I didn't have to see the recrimination on Seti's face. She might not have blamed me for Nef being taken, but she certainly blamed me for not finding her yet.

I took my time and walked slowly, telling myself it was to give me a chance to look for clues, but I really just didn't want to go back to the house. There was little I could do overnight, but it felt like I was wasting time. Running out of time.

I had to find Nef before they took her out of the city. It would be difficult to catch up if they got ahead of me on the river and if they reached Akhetaten before me, one sister would likely be dead before I found them. I had no doubt Intef would kill Nef if it was the only way he could protect the queen.

THIRTY-TWO

TEY

When I returned to Hennie's with the bucket of water, I bathed, then went straight to bed. I might have expected to sleep restlessly, but I fell into a dreamless sleep almost immediately. I woke around the middle of the night and while I waited for sleep again, I made a decision. If I didn't find Nef today, I would go to Akhetaten. I might at least be able to warn Intef before they came for his queen. I would have to take Seti with me, but if I told her I believed Nef had already been taken back to the palace, she would certainly be amenable.

When I next woke, it was to someone pounding on the front door. From the dimness of the light, I guessed it was barely dawn. Hennie and Seti stirred as I got to my feet and grabbed the two daggers I had left next to my bed mat overnight.

"Stay here," I said to them. "And keep quiet, no matter what you hear."

The person pounded again. I slipped into the main chamber and went to the door.

"Who is it?" I asked.

"Message for Tentamun," a boy said. "My captain sent me."

I unlatched the door.

"Come in, quickly."

He was probably in his early teens. Certainly old enough to work as a ship's boy. Not old enough to be an assassin looking for Seti.

"What is your message?" I asked.

"He said to tell you the man you were looking for has arrived and seeks transport. He will hold the boat as long as he can, but you should hurry."

"Does he have a girl with him?"

"I don't know. That is all my captain said."

Surely, if the captain had seen Nef, he would have included that information in his message. Perhaps she would be taken to the boat at the last minute. Someone else might be holding her nearby. Or perhaps she was already dead.

"Tell your captain I am on my way," I said.

The boy nodded and left at a quick jog. The captain must have told him to hurry. I returned to the sleeping chamber.

"I have news of the man who took Nef," I said. "I will be back when I can. Lock the door and stay inside."

"I want to go too." Seti was already up and putting on her sandals.

"No, I have to do this alone."

"Nef will be scared. She will want to see me."

"I will bring her back as soon as I have her. For now, I need you to stay here where I know you are safe."

"Nowhere is safe," Seti said bitterly. "Not for us."

Hennie wrapped her arm around Seti's shoulders.

"Come, love, we will make some breakfast. Let Tey do what she needs to. She will be able to search for Nef faster if she is on her own."

"But I want to go," Seti said.

"Seti, you are to stay here." I slipped the last of my daggers into their sheaths. "Hennie, lock the door and make sure she doesn't follow me."

As I jogged to the wharf, my thoughts were calm and my breath unhurried. I would confront the man who took Nef. If he didn't have her with him, I would make him tell me where she was. Then I would kill him. This was what I had trained for. I was ready.

Relief filled me when I reached the wharf and found the captain had been true to his word and waited for me. He stood on the deck, no doubt watching for me and wondering how much longer he could afford to wait. I crept around the edge of the wharf, keeping myself out of sight as much as possible. Nef's abductor might have accomplices watching.

Nobody seemed to pay me any attention, but as I approached the boat, the captain suddenly walked to the other end of the deck where he was shielded from sight behind the mast and the sail which was strung up and ready to be opened. It seemed he was trying to give me an opportunity to speak with him privately. Nobody else noticed as I boarded the boat.

"Your men are not very good at keeping watch," I said, as I came up behind him. "I could have a knife to your throat before they even knew I was onboard."

"True," he said. "But trained guards are expensive and I rarely have cause to worry about such a thing."

"Where is he?"

"Down below."

"Does he have a girl with him?"

"No, it is just him and his luggage, I am afraid. He booked passage for only himself, so it seems he is not expecting the girl to join him."

My heart sank. Had he already killed her? How would I ever tell Seti? How would I tell Intef I had failed him?

"Thank you for sending the boy," I said. "And for waiting."

"Of course," he said. "Go do what you must. I assume you will not require assistance?"

"No, I will do this alone. Watch for a girl. She is eight years old, almost nine, and her name is Nef, but she also answers to Neb. She must be somewhere nearby. He wouldn't leave without her."

The captain nodded and I left him there. The hatch was open and there was no way to enter without being seen. I flung myself down the ladder, using my hands to steady me but not wasting time on the steps. I landed in a crouch and was already standing as the man turned to face me.

I knew the moment he recognised me, for his face changed. He took a step back and held up his hand. As if he thought that might stop me from getting to him.

His back hit the bulkhead, and my hand was steady as I pressed my dagger against his throat.

"Where is she?" I asked.

"Who?"

"I don't have time to waste on silly games. The captain is preparing to sail and I need answers before he does."

"I don't know what you are talking about."

I removed my dagger from his throat.

"I will be reporting this—" he started.

I punched him in the belly. He doubled over, coughing and groaning. I pulled him upright by his hair and set my dagger to his throat again.

"Where is she?" I asked.

"I don't—"

I kneed him in the groin. He fell to his knees. I slammed my elbow into his back and he landed on his belly. Now I set my dagger against his ear.

"Where is she?"

"What do you want?"

I sliced downwards and took off half his ear. He screamed and clapped his hand over what was left of it. Blood ran through his fingers. I tried not to look at it.

"Where is she?"

"What kind of lunatic are you?" he cried. "I will report you to the police. You will go to prison."

"A dead man cannot report anything and you seem to be under the mistaken impression you will leave here alive."

"What do you want?" he asked.

"Every time I have to ask you where she is, I will remove a piece of your body. "

He scrambled to his feet, although not without slipping in his own blood. I let him get up.

"Where is she?"

"I know nothing."

The dagger left my hand, and its tip was buried in the bulkhead before he could move. It sliced through his other ear on the way. He screamed and now he held a hand over each ear. Blood dripped down his arms. The coppery scent of it filled the air.

"You are fortunate it went straight through your ear," I said. "Had you been standing closer to the bulkhead, it would have pinned you there."

"Son of a donkey," he screamed.

"Daughter, I think you probably mean. And speaking of girls, where is she?"

"The gods damn your house."

I knocked him off his feet. He tried to fight me, but offered little resistance. He was flat on his back as my dagger sliced through the first joint of his little finger.

He howled. It went on and on. He made so much noise, I was surprised nobody came to investigate. I assumed I could thank the captain for that.

Bile rose in my throat at the blood pouring from his hand and the sight of the tip of his finger lying on the deck. Despite all my training, this was the first time I had done something like this. I had never seen so much blood before. I steeled myself and continued.

I took two more fingers. By then, the deck was awash with blood and he was barely conscious. I wouldn't get anything else out of him.

As I wiped the blood off my daggers and slid them back into their sheaths, I remembered the captain said the man had brought luggage. Perhaps it contained a clue as to Nef's location. When I emerged from the hatch, the captain and his crew were all watching the opening. Nobody even pretended to be working. They looked me up and down, and more than one blanched at the sight of so much blood.

"I don't want any trouble," the captain said. "I was happy to help you find your daughter, but I don't need the police sniffing around my boat and looking into the goods I transport. You understand?"

"I do." My voice was steady even if my hands trembled a little. "I am afraid your passenger has injured himself. We had a bit of a tussle and he came off a little worse than me. Can you tell me where his luggage is?"

The captain waved to the boy who brought the message to Hennie's house.

"You saw what he brought on board, didn't you?" he said. "Go show her. Then you may as well get started cleaning up down there."

The boy led the way down below without a word. He paled at the sight of the body and the blood-covered deck and went no further than the bottom of the ladder. He pointed.

"That chest there is his," he said.

My heart stopped. I had expected nothing more than a couple of packs. This was sturdy and well made with a heavy wooden lock. And big enough to hold a child.

"Nef?" I pounded on the lid. "Are you in there?"

No response. I didn't know whether to hope she was there or not. If she was, she was undoubtedly dead. If she wasn't, she might be stashed somewhere in the city, perhaps waiting for someone to collect her. In a place I might never find now I had all but killed the man who knew where she was. Or she had already been smuggled out and was on her way to Akhetaten.

I had forgotten the boy until he spoke.

"Might this be useful?" He offered me an axe.

I snatched it from him, and with one strike I knocked the lock off. The latch was free. I tore open the lid and there she was.

Nef lay on her side, her legs tucked up to fit in the space. Her hands were positioned by her head. She looked peaceful, as if she had merely climbed in and fallen asleep. I lifted her out and lay her on the floor.

"I am so sorry, Nef." I brushed her hair back from her face. My fingers left bloody streaks down her cheek. "I will never forgive myself for failing you."

My tears dripped on her face and I wiped them away with my skirt. As I did, I felt the slightest puff of air on my hand. I placed my ear to her chest, but my own heart pounded too loudly for me to hear whether hers still beat. I rested my hands on her chest and felt it expand just the slightest amount as she inhaled.

She was alive.

I drew back her eyelids. Her pupils were too big. She must have been dosed with something and far too much of it. Had he intended to kill her or merely keep her quiet long enough to get her out of the city?

I scooped Nef up and carried her to the ladder. The captain was there, peering down through the hatch. Between us, we got Nef up the ladder and lay her on the deck. Fury welled within me as I looked down at her pale, unmoving figure.

"Your passenger will not be able to get up the ladder on his own," I said. "If I could have some help to get him up, I will take him to seek medical aid."

Perhaps the captain would send for the police. He might already have done so, no matter how sympathetic he had been previously. The amount of blood and the noise they heard as I interrogated the man would have been fearsome. It was not something anyone would expect to be caused by a woman.

"Of course," the captain said a little faintly. He seemed to avoid looking at me but gestured towards two of his men. "Go. Help her."

They stepped forward without complaint, although like their captain, they avoided looking at me. Between the three of us, we hauled the unconscious man up the ladder.

"Thank you," I said, once he was on the deck. "I can manage from here."

They stepped back, and I dragged the man over to the side of the boat. He was heavy, but I had spent many long hours hauling rocks that were almost too big for me to manage. I lifted him up and over the side. He splashed down into the water. I turned back to the captain and his crew.

"I am sure he will be fine once he has had medical aid," I said. "I am very sorry about all the blood."

The captain swallowed hard.

"Not to worry," he said. "The boy will clean it up. Er, we should have departed an hour ago. Do you intend to travel with us?"

"No, I need to get help for my daughter."

I lifted Nef and nodded a thank you to the captain as I carried her off the boat. My throat was too choked to speak again.

On the wharf, I lay Nef down in a shady patch. My fingers lingered on her cheek. Her skin was cold and clammy, and her lips were blue. She needed a physician and urgently. Would it be better to leave her here while I sought one or take her back to Hennie's, then go look for a physician? I found myself frozen with indecision.

THIRTY-THREE
SETI

I couldn't wait any longer. I had to know whether Tey had found Nef yet. When Grandmother wasn't watching, I tiptoed over to the door and tried to lift the bar. It was heavier than I expected and I almost couldn't do it.

"Seti, what are you doing?" Grandmother asked.

She started coming over to me. I pushed with all my might and managed to lift the bar high enough to slip it out of its fitting. I opened the door and ran.

"Seti, come back."

I could hear Grandmother running after me. But she was old and had bad knees. She couldn't run as fast as me.

It was only once I was running that I realised I didn't know how to get to the boats from Grandmother's house. I kept running anyway. Once I lost Grandmother, I could ask someone to take me to where the boats were. If I told them I was a princess, they would have to help me, and I had to find Nef. Tey mightn't look hard enough. She might give up. After all, she wasn't our real mother. She didn't love Nef the way I did, and I didn't want Nef to go to the West like Nefer and Meketaten and Merytaten.

I ran for a long time. Sweat trickled down my neck and my legs wobbled. Then suddenly I was at the wharf. I must have known the way here after all, or my feet did. I looked all around and saw Tey. She was carrying Nef off a boat. As I ran to them, she lay Nef down in the shade. Nef's arms and legs were all floppy.

"Nef!" I flung myself down beside her. I grabbed her hand and patted her cheeks, but she didn't wake up. Her skin felt funny, too cold and a little wet. I was too late.

"Nef," I sobbed. "Oh, Nef."

"Seti, what are you doing here?" Tey sounded tired, rather than angry. "You are supposed to be with Hennie."

"I came to find Nef. Is she…" My voice stopped working as I choked on a sob. "Is she dead?"

"She lives, for now at least. But I don't know how to help her. She needs a physician."

"She will be all right, won't she?"

I looked at Tey, only for a moment but long enough to see the blood all over her. Good. She deserved to get hurt for letting Nef get stolen when she was supposed to be looking after us. Nef had blood on her too, but when I poked at it, there were no hurts underneath. It was just Tey's blood. Because Tey's hands had blood all over them and she put them on my sister.

"I don't know, Seti, and that is the truth," Tey said. "She has been drugged, but I don't know what they gave her or how much. All we can do is fetch a physician and hope she is strong enough to pull through."

I gave Nef one last look, then scrubbed the tears from my eyes. Angryness welled up inside me. Somebody would pay for what they did to Nef. I would make sure of it.

I stood and turned to glare at the boat Tey took Nef from. The captain shaded his eyes with his hand as he watched us.

"You took my sister," I screamed at him.

As I looked at him, I got madder and madder. He needed to pay for what he did. Nobody paid when Nefer went to the West, but I would make sure this man paid for Nef.

The bad thing burst out of me.

Sand rose up around us, sudden and fierce.

"Seti." Tey tried to grab my arm, but I shook her off. "Seti, you need to calm down."

"Son of a donkey," I cried to the captain. "You are worth less than a fly standing in dog excrement. You..." I couldn't think of any other bad things to call him. "I hope Aten destroys your house."

"Seti, you know what happens when you get mad." Tey grabbed my shoulders and turned me to face her. "You promised you wouldn't do this again."

"He took her," I yelled right at Tey's face. The bad thing was already out. It was too late to stop it and I didn't even care. "He took Nef."

"He didn't, Seti."

I twisted around to stare at the captain. In my head, I told the bad thing to go get him. To make him pay.

The sandstorm grew bigger and bigger.

It reached the boat.

The boat rocked and the people on board grabbed hold of anything they could find to stop themselves from falling over. Waves splashed, kicked up by the storm racing around the boat.

"Seti, stop this immediately," Tey yelled.

Sand whirled around me. From the corner of my eye, I could see Tey covering Nef with her own body. The sand spun and danced around us. It spun around the boat, too.

The boat tilted and just faintly over the sound of the wind, I heard the cries from the people on board. A cloud of sand flung itself against the boat and it tilted in the other direction. Someone or something landed in the water with a splash.

"Seti, you have to stop," Tey called. "You will kill someone."

"Yes," I said. "He took Nef. He is going to be very sorry."

"No, he didn't. Seti, listen to me."

But the bad thing wanted me to give in to it. To let it grow even bigger. So I let it feel how angry I was and I let it go.

The wind got stronger and its howl drowned out Tey's shouts.

The boat tipped again and this time it kept tipping until it fell right over. The crew scrambled to get clear.

As the boat sank, I suddenly wasn't angry anymore. The bad thing went back down my throat and into my belly. The wind dropped and sand fell from the air.

The hair in Nef's sidelock was coming out of its braid and was all out of place. I brushed it back from her face as I watched the crew hauling themselves from the water. I hoped the captain was dead.

"Dear Aten. What happened?"

Grandmother had arrived. She was panting and red-faced. She must have run after me.

"How much did you see?" Tey asked.

"Just the boat sinking," Grandmother said. "What in the god's name happened here?"

Before Tey could say anything, Grandmother saw Nef.

"Oh, sweet child." She dropped down beside Nef. "Is she…"

"Alive, but barely," Tey said. "She needs a physician. Take her home and I will go find one."

"Come, Seti," Grandmother said. "Between you and me, we will be able to carry your sister."

I tore my gaze from the water. I hadn't seen the captain since the boat sank.

Tey grabbed my arm and held it very tightly. It hurt and I whimpered, but she didn't let go.

"That was wrong, Seti," she said. "Very wrong. Those people did nothing."

"They took Nef. They deserved it."

"They didn't take her. They didn't even know she was on board. The captain helped me find her. He is the one who sent the boy this morning."

I looked from Tey to the boat. I didn't understand.

"So, where is the man who took her?" I asked.

"Dead. I fed him to the crocodiles."

I turned back to the river.

"But the captain…"

"Did nothing but help me. He kept the boat at the wharf to give me time to get here so I could find Nef. You did a very bad thing."

I didn't know what to say. "Nef."

"Yes, help Hennie take her home. I will be there as soon as I can."

Between Grandmother and me, we lifted Nef. Grandmother was still puffing and heaving, and I didn't think she would be able to go very far without stopping to rest. Tey ran off to find a physician.

We never should have left the palace. If we were still there, we could have sent a runner to find the royal physician. He would know how to fix Nef. What if Tey couldn't find anyone here who could?

THIRTY-FOUR

TEY

I stopped to ask a couple of people where I could find a physician, but nobody knew. One told me of a woman who sold potions in the market and someone else knew of a midwife. I ran to the market. There would be lots of people there at this time of day. Surely somebody would know a physician. Eventually, I found a man who gave me directions to the physician's house.

To my relief, the physician was at home and he needed little persuasion once I assured him I could pay.

"What are her symptoms?" he asked, snatching up a basket and filling it with an assortment of items from a shelf.

"She breathes shallowly. Her pupils are dilated and her lips are blue."

"Unconscious?" He frowned at his medicines, then selected another.

"Yes. She hasn't moved since I found her."

"Do you know how long she has been in this state?"

"No."

"And you do not have any information about what she has been dosed with?"

"No."

"Hmm." He grabbed another couple of items. "Show me the way."

We walked briskly back to Hennie's house. I would have run all the way, but there was no point leaving the physician behind and the fellow seemed willing to go no faster than a quick walk. Seti was waiting at the door when we arrived.

They had laid Nef out on her bed mat. Hennie was sponging her face and limbs, but moved aside to give the physician room.

"Has she woken at all?" the physician asked.

He knelt beside Nef and pulled up her eyelids.

"Not even briefly," Hennie said.

The physician checked her breath and her tongue, then counted her heartbeats. It was only when he raised her hand to study her fingers that I noticed how blue the tips were, just like her lips. He pinched and poked at her skin and did a few other things I couldn't see the point of. Presumably, he knew what he was doing. At length, he withdrew a small bottle from his basket.

"I suspect she has been dosed with poppy," he said. "She has had far too much, though, and I must warn you she might not survive, especially if they gave her multiple doses to keep her unconscious."

The physician tipped a few drops from the bottle onto Nef's tongue, then retrieved an assortment of other items from his basket. He prayed and chanted as he placed magical amulets over her chest and on the places where her liver and kidneys were. He handed Hennie a bundle of herbs. I didn't recognise any of them.

"You should burn these," he said. "Move the child to where she will be able to breathe in the smoke. Close the shutters and put blankets over them to ensure the smoke stays inside for as long as possible. Then you should cook her favourite foods and lay them out beside her. If there is a particular flower she likes, pick as many as you can and place them on her chest and belly."

"What will all that do?" I asked.

"It may help to call her back from wherever she wanders. She has one foot in the underworld already. You must remind her of the things she loves in this world in order to entice her to return."

"Will she come back?"

He looked down at Nef and frowned.

"She may or she may not," he said. "I have done all I can. It is up to her what she chooses now."

He packed up his basket and it was clear his consultation was finished. I offered him one of the bags of barley I had given Hennie. He hefted it in his hand, considering its weight, then nodded and left.

I had forgotten Seti until she let out a sob.

"She will wake up, won't she?" she asked.

"We need to do everything the physician said," Hennie said briskly. "We will give her the best possible chance. Seti, dear, there is a small brazier in the other chamber. Go fetch it for me and we will get the herbs burning. Tey, perhaps you could close the shutters and pin up some blankets. I will go out to the garden and pick some flowers as soon as we get the brazier going."

I did that, then went to the door.

"Where are you going?" Seti asked. "You need to stay with Nef."

"There is nothing more I can do for her right now," I said. "I need to go back to the wharf and see if I can help down there."

Seti turned back to Nef without comment. Did she still not understand the magnitude of what she had done? She might well have killed someone with her storm. If nothing else, she had destroyed the captain's livelihood. Much like I killed the farmer who had done nothing but spy on us. We had both acted without having enough information. Perhaps when I was less angry at her, I might feel more sympathetic, but right now, my fury overshadowed anything else. I could barely look at her.

"You go, dear," Hennie said. "Seti and I can look after things here."

I ran back to the wharf. It was still in chaos. People were retrieving items from the water. A couple of boys dived to snatch up what they could from the bottom of the river, or at least the parts they could reach. Some of the crew lay on the wharf and for a moment, I feared they were dead. But one of them turned his head to the side, and another seemed to talk, so perhaps they were only injured.

I helped where I could, taking items the diving boys passed up and carrying them over to where the salvaged items were laid out. At length, there seemed to be nothing else to retrieve. The injured crew had disappeared by now, likely having been carried back to their homes or other accommodation, and the crowd of onlookers had thinned. I spotted the captain.

His shoulders slumped and his eyes were weary as he nodded at me.

"How is the girl?" he asked.

"It is too soon to tell. The physician has seen her, but he doesn't know whether she will survive."

"I am very unhappy my boat was used to steal her away. For that, I am sorry. It is not something I would have allowed, had I known."

"You did nothing but help me," I said. "I am very grateful for that and I am so sorry for what happened. It is…" I couldn't find the words to express my horror at what Seti had done.

"I have never seen a storm like that before," he said. "But I have heard of such things, where the wind suddenly forms a tunnel and sweeps everything from the ground. I never thought to live through such a thing myself."

"Your boat. I am sorry."

He turned back to the river and sighed.

"It is gone and that is all I can say," he said. "I don't know what I will do now."

"I just… I am so sorry."

"The whim of the gods is a strange thing," he said. "Perhaps this is a punishment. I have tried to live a good life, but maybe it was not good enough. Perhaps Aten felt I should have been more discriminating about what cargo I transported. Had I realised earlier the chest contained a child, maybe this would not have happened. I knew you were looking for her. I should have figured it out."

Realisation dawned. He didn't know it was Seti. He thought the storm was sent by the gods. I didn't know whether to be relieved or horrified or something else. I could only hope that if anyone saw Seti before the storm, they would think she was merely a child having a tantrum and would, like the captain, think the gods were to blame.

THIRTY-FIVE

TEY

Since there was nothing else I could do to help at the wharf, I went back to Hennie's house. I had never known a day to pass more slowly. It was as if time stood still while Seti, Hennie and I waited at Nef's side. The bitter aroma of the herbs was overpowering at first, but after a while, I hardly noticed them.

The chamber was far too warm with the brazier burning and the shutters closed, and sweat trickled down my neck and back. Nef's skin was flushed and damp, but I couldn't tell whether she had a fever or was just hot. From time to time, I tiptoed over to the window to raise the blanket just the tiniest bit and check how far across the sky the sun had travelled. It was the only thing that told me time really did pass.

At one point, Nef's chest seemed to still, and I held my breath as I prayed Aten would let her live. After a few moments, she breathed again and I finally let out my own breath as well. I glanced at Seti, wondering whether she had noticed, but she seemed to be staring down at Nef's hand, which she clutched in her own. She must have felt my gaze on her, for she looked up and caught my eye.

"How much longer?" she whispered.

I shook my head but couldn't find a reply for her. Anger at her careless act welled up inside me and if I said anything to her right now, it would probably be something I would regret once my temper cooled.

"It is impossible to say, dear," Hennie said. "Perhaps you should speak to Nef. If she wanders towards the West, the voice of someone she loves might call her back."

"What would I talk about?" Seti asked.

"Anything you like. Memories, perhaps. Your childhood together."

Seti shot me a look, as if asking for permission.

"Hennie knows the truth," I said. "Besides, you already told her you were princesses."

I didn't even try to hide the bitterness in my voice. After all I had done to protect them, everything I had given up, Seti told the first person she could.

Seti didn't seem to notice the recrimination in my voice. As much as I didn't want to listen to what she said to Nef, there was no way to avoid it, given we were all crammed into a chamber together. Seti spoke of their lives as princesses and about mischief they had gotten into. About chasing ducks in their mother's pleasure garden. About fleeing their tutor and hiding in an unused chamber while the fellow mobilised the queen's personal squad to search for them.

She talked about their sister who was now a queen, and more briefly about their other sisters. Seti must have been very young when they went to the West and likely she barely remembered them, if at all, although there seemed to be one she still held particular fondness for. She spoke about their father, who had gone to the West just a couple of months ago, and also about their mother, her memories of whom already faded. At last, her chatter stilled.

"That is everything, Nef," she said. "That is all I can remember. So you have to wake up now because I have no more memories to tell you."

"You did very well, dear." Hennie's voice was choked and she cleared her throat. She wrapped her arm around Seti and drew her closer.

"Do you think she heard me?" Seti asked.

"I have no doubt of it. Whether it will be enough to call her back, we will have to wait and see."

An hour passed, then another. The chamber grew darker and Hennie slipped out to fetch a lamp and some food.

"Eat," she said when she returned with a tray. "You must both be hungry and you need to keep up your strength."

I wasn't hungry, but my mouth was dry and I gratefully accepted a mug of beer. It was thick and a little salty and my stomach stirred in response. Perhaps I could eat after all. Hennie had brought slices of grainy bread with cucumbers and little sweet onions from her own garden. The vegetables were crisp and although the bread was from yesterday, it made a tasty enough meal.

Seti nibbled on a few slices of cucumber, but shook her head when Hennie pressed her to eat more. She gave me a few sidelong glances as if waiting for me to encourage her, but I ignored her.

Nothing had turned out the way I imagined it would. I thought my skills would be enough to keep them safe, but I failed. I was angry at Seti, but in truth, I was just as mad at myself. I had suspected the fellow was watching me, but didn't let myself trust my instincts and I was too slow to react. How ashamed Papa would be if he knew what a mess I had made.

As we sat by Nef's side through the night, I began to plan. There were decisions to be made. If Nef went to the West, should I take Seti away? Or should I return to Akhetaten to take back word of her death? Could I entrust such news to a messenger? And if she survived, there would be even more decisions. Do I continue with the journey? Do I take them both home and admit I had failed? Do I just kill them and be done with it all? I considered that last option for far longer than I would have admitted to anyone. If the princesses were dead, they couldn't be used against the queen. Since Seti seemed determined to sabotage my attempts to keep them safe by using this strange ability she wasn't willing to admit she even had, what else could I do?

Perhaps I had been wrong to think this task was my destiny. All my life I had been certain I would one day do something important, and when the opportunity arose to take the princesses to safety, I didn't hesitate. I thought this was what I had been preparing for. But I had failed — miserably. Either this wasn't my destiny after all or I wasn't as good as I thought I was. Perhaps both those things were true.

Nef stirred a little and my morose thoughts fled.

"Nef?" Seti leaned over to peer into her face. "Are you awake?"

When Nef didn't respond, Seti shook her shoulders.

"Nef!"

"Seti, dear, give her time." Hennie pulled her back.

Nef groaned and moved her head the tiniest bit. Then she opened her eyes.

Seti burst into tears.

Nef looked at each of us and opened her mouth, but didn't seem to be able to talk.

"Just wait, dear." Hennie brought her a mug of beer. "Tey, lift her shoulders so she can drink. Her throat is likely too parched to speak."

I held Nef up and Hennie lifted the mug to her mouth, setting the reed straw against her lips. Nef drank thirstily and when I lowered her back down again, she looked a little more awake.

"What happened?" Her voice was scratchy and uneven.

"What do you remember?" I asked.

She frowned and shook her head.

"I don't know," she said. "I am too hot. Am I ill?"

"We closed up the chamber to keep in the scent of the herbs burning on the brazier," I said. "The physician said to do it."

She closed her eyes and I thought she had fallen asleep.

"There was a man," she said at last. "He grabbed me. I was getting water from the well. Seti and I were playing in the garden. He made me drink something. It tasted bad and I didn't want it.

Hennie asked us to go get water. The man jumped out from an alley. Seti wanted to keep playing, so I went by myself."

Her memories were clearly out of order, but I gleaned enough to understand the fellow had jumped out at her while she was fetching water. He made her drink something, and that was how he drugged her.

"Don't worry about what you can or cannot remember," I said. "You are safe now and that is all that matters."

"Did you find my sandals? I kicked them off. I thought..." Her voice failed and Hennie made me raise Nef up again so she could drink some more. "I thought you might find me if I left a clue."

"I found them. You did well to think of that. It was what made me certain you had been taken rather than lost or run away."

"Sorry, Tey." Her voice was so quiet, I could hardly hear her. "You taught us how to get away, but I was too scared. I couldn't remember."

"Don't worry about it. We got you back."

"I am so tired. I just want to sleep."

We removed the brazier and left the door to the other chamber open to let the air cool a little. Seti pushed her bed mat over so she could lie close enough to hold Nef's hand.

Hennie and I went out to the other chamber. She dropped onto the rug with a sigh and seemed to stare at nothing. I was tired, but I prowled the chamber restlessly. I needed to make a decision.

"Sit down, dear," Hennie said. "Whatever you are grappling with can surely wait until tomorrow."

I sat on the rug and stared at my hands.

"I suppose you will take them away now," she said.

"I am trying to decide. It is no longer safe here for them. I don't know whether the man who took Nef told anyone else he had found them. When he doesn't return with her, more might follow."

"Do you know why he only took Nef?"

"He wouldn't tell me anything. I presume he meant to take her back to Akhetaten so they could put her on the throne."

"Why not take Seti too, then? Or why not kill her if they only needed one princess?"

"I don't know. Perhaps they planned to keep her in reserve. If their attempt with Nef was unsuccessful, they knew where to find Seti."

"Assuming she was still here."

"They might have thought I would stay here hoping Nef would somehow escape and make her way back. Maybe they are still watching and will follow if we leave. Maybe once they had Nef on the throne, someone would have come to kill Seti."

"How heartless. Would they really kill an innocent girl?"

I ducked my head so Hennie couldn't see the guilt on my face. It was no more than I had considered myself. I was a coward. The job was harder than I expected and I hadn't done it as well as I anticipated, so I wanted to give up. Papa would be ashamed if he knew I had even considered such a thing.

"We will leave as soon as Nef can travel," I said.

"Where will you go?"

"I don't know. Best that you know nothing anyway. Someone may come after us. There might be questions."

"And they will kill me when I cannot give them the answers they need."

Regret filled me as I realised the situation we had put Hennie in. If someone had discovered where the girls had been living, she was in just as much danger as we were. Whether she knew anything or not was irrelevant. They would think she did and they wouldn't hesitate to torture her to get the information they needed.

"We will come up with a story for you," I said. "Something you can tell anyone who comes asking after us. They will think you have told them everything you know."

"And then they will kill me for it." Her voice was calm. "They will not leave me alive to share the same information with anyone who follows after them. You know this, Tey. I still don't understand how a woman was given the task of protecting two princesses, but you have clearly been well trained in preparation. I am sure you do not doubt that anyone who comes looking for the girls after you leave will kill me without a second thought."

"I am so sorry. I would never have brought them here if I thought something like this would happen. I thought I was careful enough that nobody could have followed us."

"What is done is done," she said briskly. "All that matters now is what you will do about it."

"The girls have some gems from their mother. You could take one and go away. Make a new life for yourself somewhere far away."

"You would send an old woman away to travel alone?" she asked. "An old woman who has no ability to defend herself the way you do?"

"What else would you suggest?"

"I will come with you, if you will have me. Those girls... they have come to feel like family. I love them as if they truly were my own granddaughters. If you will let an old woman travel with you, I will go wherever you take them."

THIRTY-SIX

TEY

I didn't give Hennie an answer that night. I couldn't. I didn't know whether I could keep the princesses safe, let alone her as well. Hennie went off to bed a little while later. I lay on the rug and dozed a little, but mostly I just listened for intruders. It would only be a matter of time before the next person came for them.

By morning, Nef was able to sit up. I went to the well to fetch water so she could bathe, although not without instructing Hennie to lock the door behind me and keep the shutters latched until I returned. I walked briskly and kept very close watch for anyone following me, but saw nothing suspicious.

While Nef bathed and Hennie was busy with some housework, I sat Seti down on the rug.

"We need to talk about what happened," I said.

"Nef woke up." She beamed at me.

"Not that. What you did at the wharf."

Seti's smile disappeared and she frowned a little.

"Do you understand what you did?" I asked.

She looked away, tears trembling, and when she answered, her voice was very small.

"I don't want to talk about it."

"We have to talk about it. I need to know you understand it was wrong."

"They took Nef. I wanted them to be sorry."

"The man who took her had already been punished. I took care of it. What you did was hurt a lot of innocent people. The boat you sank was the captain's livelihood."

"He shouldn't have taken Nef."

"Seti, the captain didn't take Nef. I have already told you this. She was taken onboard his boat secretly and he didn't even know she was there."

She shook her head and wiped away a few tears that spilled down her cheeks.

"Tell me how you made the storm," I said.

She was silent.

"Seti."

"I don't know. It just happens."

"When you get mad about something."

"When I get mad, sometimes the bad thing gets out."

"What is the bad thing?"

"I don't know," she whispered.

"Can you control it? Can you make the wind stronger or slower?"

Seti shook her head.

"It is not the wind," she said. "It is the sand. When I get mad, the bad thing makes the sand move."

"Seti, I need you to promise me you won't let it happen again. We will work on some techniques you can use to calm yourself when you get angry, but I need your word you will do your best to make sure something like this never happens again."

"It is not my fault," she said. "The bad thing does it."

"The gods have given you a special ability. I have never even heard of such a thing before, but maybe we can find someone who can teach you how to control it. How to harness it. But until then, you must promise me you won't use it."

She shrugged and looked away. Frustration surged through me. She still didn't understand the impact of her actions.

"Seti, you sank the captain's boat. That boat was how he earns his income, how he feeds his family, and he was innocent."

"He really didn't take Nef?"

I swallowed my sigh of frustration. Perhaps she was too young to understand.

"No, I swear to you. He had nothing to do with what happened to Nef. In fact, he helped me find her. Remember how it was the captain who sent a boy to tell me he had found the man I was looking for? The one who took Nef."

She stared down at her hands and didn't reply.

I didn't think she was just being obstinate. She truly didn't seem to understand. I could make amends to the captain, though. I had the little pouch of gems Intef took from their mother's collection. When I slipped into the other chamber, Nef was sleeping again, or at least lying with her eyes closed. I took the pouch from where I wore it around my waist under my shirt. I hadn't looked inside it before. Perhaps there wouldn't be anything that would be of value to the captain.

But when I tipped the jewels into my palm, I gasped. Until this moment, I had no idea how much wealth it contained. Once we found a safe place to live, the gems in these jewels would surely fund a lifestyle that was equivalent to what the princesses were used to. I selected the two finest finger rings — a series of rubies set in a silver band and a large blue sapphire.

As I slipped out the door, Seti called to me.

"Nef?" she said. "Are you going to the captain?"

"I am."

I was tempted to tell her I intended to give the man two of the gems that were intended for her and Nef. But it would be better if the girls didn't know about them. Not yet, anyway. Aten only knew who Seti might tell if she knew about the wealth I carried on their behalf.

"Will you tell him I am sorry?" Seti asked in a very small voice.

"Of course."

I could hardly relay her apology without telling the captain that Seti was responsible for the storm. Better that he continued to think it was the will of the gods. The last thing we needed was rumours about a girl with a strange ability. There was already reason enough for people to search for us.

I found the captain in a drinking house. Despite the early hour, he had obviously been there for some time. He reeked of red wine and sweat, and didn't look up when I stood beside him. It was only after I sat that I realised I still didn't know what to say to him.

"Well then," he said at last. "Have you come to tell me the girl who was smuggled onto my boat has gone to the West?"

"No, she has survived. It looks like she will recover with no ill effects."

"Well, the gods were good to someone, at least."

"Have you recovered anything else from the boat?"

"Have not been back to the wharf since yesterday. No point. My boat is too far under the water for any chance of recovery."

"What will you do now?"

He stared blearily down into his mug.

"No idea," he said. "I need to find work or I cannot support my family. Labouring perhaps. My wife is an adequate seamstress. She might have to take in some sewing, although the gods only know how she will find time for such a thing. She is busy enough with raising six children and baking bread and brewing beer enough for us all. But she will have to manage because there are not enough hours of daylight for me to labour enough to feed so many mouths."

I opened my hand and showed him the gems.

"Would these be sufficient to replace your boat?" I asked.

His eyes widened and he seemed to struggle to speak.

"I know little about the worth of such items," he said, "but I suspect they would replace my boat several times over."

"Take them then. Buy a new boat so you can support your family."

He shot me a cautious look. He seemed more sober now.

"How did you come by such wealth?" he asked. "Did you steal them?"

"They were a gift." That was true enough.

"So why not keep them for yourself? You and your daughters could live off them for the rest of your lives. Why give them to a stranger?"

"I would not have found my daughter if you hadn't sent your boy. I want you to have them. We will manage well enough."

The captain shook his head.

"I cannot take your wealth," he said.

I set the gems down beside his hand.

"Take them," I said. "I am very grateful for your help."

I left before he could say anything else. I doubted he would walk away and leave the gems lying there for someone else. He might not want to take them from me, but he was no fool.

THIRTY-SEVEN

TEY

W hen I reached Hennie's home, Nef was out of bed. She was pale and had the strength to do no more than sit on a cushion, but it was an improvement.

"How long until she can travel, do you think?" I asked Hennie when I was sure I was out of earshot of both girls.

"Days at least. Maybe a couple of weeks. She is very weak."

"I cannot afford to wait that long. Is there anything we can do to help her recover faster? A tonic from the physician or something?"

"I suppose there are strengthening tonics, but time is the best medicine for her right now. Surely the girls are safe inside the house. We will keep the door locked and the shutters closed."

"If anyone else knows where we are, all the locked doors in the world won't keep them away. The men who want to find them have Pharaoh's army at their disposal. A door will be little barrier for a squad of soldiers. They will take the house apart if they have to. If they come for us, they *will* get the girls."

"And what will they do with them if they find them? If they intended to kill Nef, they would have done it right away. You said yourself they meant to take her back to the palace. Perhaps that would be better for Nef than a lifetime of running away."

"That doesn't mean she is safe. If they take her back, there are other men — men loyal to the throne — who would kill her to protect the queen." And those men might include my brother. "Remember, they only need one of the three sisters alive. No matter which of them is on the throne, the other two are disposable. If they make Nef queen, they will send someone else to kill Seti."

"So you believe the only way to keep them both safe is to take them away from here?"

"It is not just these two I am trying to keep safe, but the queen as well. As long as nobody can find her sisters, they need her. She is the highest ranked princess of their mother's bloodline and it is marriage to her that makes Pharaoh legitimate."

"I had hoped there might be a way to give the girls some stability. Endless travel is no life for young children."

"It won't be endless travel. I just need to get them far enough away to be safe."

"But where do we travel to? Tell me you have a plan."

"I have been wracking my brain to come up with something," I said. "But before I say anything more, are you certain you want to come with us?"

"These girls have given me a new life and I cannot imagine how long and empty the days would be without them. They have brought laughter back to a lonely old woman. Wherever you intend to take them, I will go with you."

"It gives us a better cover story anyway. By now, it seems there must be other people who know the girls travel with a sole female. If we also have their grandmother with us, nobody who searches for a woman and two girls will look twice."

"So where do we go then? I was thinking maybe north? There are lots of villages there, from what I hear."

"North means we would have to pass Akhetaten," I said. "And I think that is too risky. It would only take one person to glimpse a face they recognise to leave a trail for someone to follow. I think we should continue south."

"But to where? There is not much of Egypt south of Nubet."

"We will go to Nubia for now." We couldn't stay there. Papa

and Intef had considered Nubia, which meant others would think of it too. "Past Nubia, maybe even to Punt."

"Is that not obvious, though? They have already tracked you travelling south. When they cannot find us, won't they assume we have continued south?"

"So where then? Our options are north or south. There is only desert to the east and west."

Hennie and I looked at each other, and the same thought must have occurred to her as to me.

"They won't expect us to travel into the desert," I said.

"But how would we survive out there?"

"We only need to survive long enough to cross the desert. We can go to the coast."

"The coast?" Hennie's voice was doubtful. "That is an awfully long way."

"Fifty leagues. Maybe sixty. But think about it, Hennie. If we can get to the Red Sea, food will be easy. We can fish and catch crabs and sea birds. Rock oysters, sand rats, eggs from the sea birds."

"But where would we live?"

"We will find a cave, or I will build us a house. We don't need much, just shelter in bad weather. I think the girls would be happy there. Can you not picture them? Splashing in the ocean, building villages in the sand."

"It sounds idyllic." Hennie gave me a small smile. "It is a very long way to travel, though."

"We wouldn't walk, of course. We will buy some donkeys, and there must be a known route across the desert. Places with wells or oases. We will not be the first people to travel in such a place."

"But if you ask around, won't that leave a trail someone might follow?"

"I will do it carefully. I will go out this afternoon and start purchasing supplies. In the meantime, I need you to brew as much beer as you think we can travel with and bake many loaves of bread. Something hard that will travel well. Tell me what supplies you need."

Seti wandered in and we left off our conversation. I didn't want them to know yet. They wouldn't be happy about leaving, even once they learnt Hennie would be coming, and I wasn't sure I could trust Seti not to stir up the sand, or whatever it was her "bad thing" did.

Hennie asked about Nef and Seti responded briefly without looking at either her or me. She seemed sullen, or perhaps upset. Maybe she was starting to understand the gravity of what she had done.

THIRTY-EIGHT

SETI

I tried not to listen when Tey said the captain wasn't the man who took Nef. It made me feel bad every time she said it, which she did over and over. I didn't believe her at first. I saw her carrying Nef off the boat with my own eyes. But Tey kept saying it wasn't the captain's fault. She said she already killed the bad man before I got there.

But the bad thing sank the captain's boat. It wasn't my fault — I couldn't control the bad thing — but when I let myself believe Tey, I felt horrible. Maybe I should have tried harder not to let the bad thing out.

What would happen to me if anyone else found out what I had done? Would Tey tell someone? Maybe now she knew about the bad thing she would take us back to Akhetaten. She would give us to Ankhesenpaaten and tell her to let the bad men have us because I had a bad thing inside me. Or maybe she would kill me. Nef didn't have a bad thing, so Tey wouldn't kill her. Or maybe she would. Then she could do whatever she wanted because she wouldn't have to look after us anymore.

I felt sad when I thought about how Tey might not want us anymore. She wasn't as mean as I thought she was to start with. Sometimes she even smiled. She never looked happy, though, so I didn't think she liked Nef and me much. She probably couldn't wait to get rid of us and now she knew about the bad thing, she had the perfect excuse. Ankhesenpaaten wouldn't expect Tey to keep protecting us if she knew about the bad thing.

Nef was getting a little bit better every day. We didn't talk much. She said it made her too tired. I asked if she had been listening when I told her all my memories, but she didn't seem to know what I was talking about.

Tey and Grandmother were spending a lot of time whispering together. They stopped when I came near them, so whatever they were talking about, they didn't want me to know. Maybe they were making plans about how Tey could get rid of us. Nef and I should run away before they had time to do whatever they were planning.

As soon as Nef could walk without getting too tired, that is what we would do. We would go somewhere where nobody knew about the bad thing or that we used to be princesses. That way, nobody would want to kill us anymore.

THIRTY-NINE

TEY

Two weeks passed while Nef recovered and Hennie and I made arrangements to leave. I itched at the delay, but there was nothing to be done for it. We needed to be thoroughly prepared before we left. The travelling would be far more difficult than sailing from Akhetaten. In truth, I wasn't convinced travelling across the desert was a good plan, but it was the only one I had. Every day we delayed brought the next attack a day closer.

I had intended to tell the girls only at the last possible moment, but as soon as they saw the pile of supplies stacked against the wall separating the two chambers, they grew suspicious.

"We are leaving soon, aren't we?" Nef asked as we ate our evening meal. She was finally strong enough to leave her bed mat and sit with us to eat.

Hennie and I looked at each other. I knew she waited for me to tell them, but for a moment I hoped she might do it.

"We have to," I said. "If one man knows where we are, others undoubtedly do, too."

"Are we going home, then?" she asked. "Since the bad men have found us anyway, there is no point staying away."

The bread in my throat suddenly became too dry and I swallowed with difficulty.

"We cannot go back to Akhetaten, Nef," I said. "I thought you understood that."

"I just thought we might be able to now," she said.

I tried to find the right words.

"Now they know where we are, it is more important than ever that we disappear. Your sister trusted me to keep you safe and I cannot do that here anymore."

"But where will we go?" Nef asked.

I glanced at Seti, wondering why she hadn't said anything yet. She was the one who had the most difficulty with understanding why they couldn't go home. But Seti stared down at her plate, her mouth pursed into something that might have been a frown or might have been moments away from bursting into tears.

"I don't know yet," I said.

It was better they didn't know our destination. If somebody snatched one of the princesses again, they couldn't tell what they didn't know. I might yet keep the other safe if that happened.

"I don't want to go," Seti said.

She shot me a glare and I knew her well enough to know she was on the edge of a tantrum.

"Seti, you need to stay calm," I said. "Remember what we talked about? Breathe, just like we practised the other day. In and out."

She glowered at me, but she took a few deep breaths.

"I don't want to leave Grandmother," Nef said with a sniffle. "I like being here with her."

"That is the best part." Hennie patted Nef's hand. "I am coming with you."

"You are?" Nef asked.

Both girls seemed to brighten. I felt a little insulted they had never acted that pleased to have me with them, but I pushed the emotion away and concentrated on my planning. After being wrenched away from everything they knew, it was only natural the girls would cling to someone who treated them as if they were her own granddaughters.

As the day approached for us to leave, I couldn't focus on anything. I paced the chambers, irritating the girls as they played on the floor with the little wooden men Hennie's husband had made when Menna was a boy, and getting in Hennie's way as she tried to decide what to pack and what to leave behind.

Other than the possibility of somebody finding us before we could leave, my biggest concern was getting to the coast. Even with donkeys, it would take at least a couple of weeks. Maybe more. We could carry food enough for that long, and we could ration our supplies if they grew short, but having enough to drink was the bigger problem.

It wasn't just us who would need to drink, but the donkeys, too. I wasn't sure we could carry enough beer for us and also enough water for the donkeys. And the more donkeys we took, the more food and water we needed for them. I spent several days trying to calculate how much we needed to carry. Like most girls, I had no schooling, but Papa taught me what he could, although it was only the basics of reading and some very simple sums. This kind of calculation was far more complicated than anything I knew how to do.

"We need twenty-five *hinw* of beer for us and sixty-three *hinw* of water for each donkey," I said to Hennie. "We cannot travel with that sort of quantity."

"I thought you expected to find oases along the way," she said. "Even if we only find one, that means we need only carry half as much as you have calculated."

"Dare we risk it, though? What if we count on finding water and we never do?"

"You are worrying needlessly. Are there not tribes who live in the desert? There must be water out there or they couldn't live in such a place."

"The desert is vast. I am certain there are oases, and yes, the Sand Wanderers live out there somewhere, but what if we cannot find water? The place is so big we might well spend a month travelling and not encounter either an oasis or any person."

"You said you knew how to find water in the desert. I trust you will get us through it."

"I know how to find enough water for me to survive on. That is different from being able to find water enough for the four of us, plus fifteen donkeys."

"As our supplies grow low, we will not need so many donkeys. We can slaughter the beasts as they become surplus, and they will provide extra food for us as well as reducing how much water we need. Tey, dear, I think you are worrying too much. We will make it."

"I will never forgive myself if I lead the girls out into the desert, only for them to perish. I am supposed to be keeping them safe."

"And keeping them safe is exactly what you will do. Tey, it is not like you to be so filled with doubt. What is this really about?"

I sighed and studied my calculations again. I had covered Hennie's wall with little charcoal pictures representing each donkey and how much food and water we needed for it. Then I painstakingly counted them all up. It was the only way I could figure out such a calculation and I still wasn't sure I had it right.

"They already got Nef once," I said. "She nearly didn't survive."

I left my calculations and resumed pacing. The girls were being quiet, and I glanced into the other chamber to make sure they were still there. They sat together on Nef's bed mat and seemed to be talking.

"And you blame yourself for that," Hennie said.

There was no judgement in her words, just an observation.

"I do. I have told you that."

"But are you not also responsible for saving her? If you hadn't found her, they would have taken her away and Aten only knows what would have become of her then."

I had no response for that. My eventual rescue of Nef didn't outweigh the fact that she was taken in the first place.

"I think Nef will be ready to travel within the next couple of days."

Hennie had obviously figured she would not persuade me and may as well change the subject.

"Yes, she has been looking much stronger. I think we should leave as soon as possible. We could probably leave tomorrow morning except that it will take me a full day to fetch enough water for the donkeys."

"Best not to rush it," she said. "Another day of rest can only do her good. But as for the donkeys, why don't we take them all to the well and fill their water containers in one trip?"

"I didn't want to be so conspicuous. If anyone comes looking for us, and I have no doubt they will, fifteen donkeys at the well is something folk will remember."

"So we take them at night," Hennie suggested. "After folk have gone to sleep."

I considered it.

"They will make an awful lot of noise, though. You know how sound travels at night."

"We can skirt around the town. Keep to the edges of the paddocks. There is another well, further than the one we use, but closer to the edge of town. If you think it is that urgent, we could take them tonight, then leave immediately so nobody sees us coming back."

"I suppose. We have everything ready except the water."

"The last batch of beer could use another day or two to brew, but it will be good enough. I will bake more bread this afternoon so we have a few fresh loaves, but there is nothing else that needs to be done."

"I will go tell the man I bought the donkeys from that we will need them tonight. I will have to bring some of them back here for our supplies. Then we can collect the others, go to the well, and be off."

"It is as good a plan as any," Hennie said.

"This is your last chance to change your mind. Are you sure you want to leave your life here behind?"

"I don't see it as leaving my life behind, dear. You and the girls are my life now. I am merely moving on with you."

FORTY

TEY

I spent the afternoon bringing the donkeys in pairs to Hennie's home and loading them up. The farmer regularly supplied travellers and he had been able to provide everything we needed in terms of halters for the donkeys and pairs of baskets joined in such a way that they could be draped over a beast's back so it carried a basket on each side. He showed me how to fasten the donkeys to long ropes to ensure none wandered away. Every donkey would carry either supplies or a person, and we couldn't afford to lose a single one.

As we ate our last meal in Hennie's home, I wondered whether this would be the final evening of normalcy for the girls. I prayed to Aten I wasn't leading them into a worse situation.

"Nef," I said. "Seti. We are leaving tonight. Once you are finished eating, I need you to pack up your things and get ready to go."

"Tonight?" Nef asked. "You mean, while it is dark?"

"As soon as the moon rises, we will go," I said.

"But when will we sleep?" Seti asked. "I am tired. I don't want to leave tonight."

"We must, Seti," I said. "Our supplies are all ready and the donkeys are waiting for us."

They already knew we would travel by donkey, although I had not told them we were going into the desert. Nef was initially excited about riding, but Seti's sourness had rubbed off on her.

"Do the donkeys smell?" Nef asked.

"They smell like donkeys," I said.

"Ew," Seti said. "I bet they will make me smell bad."

"Have you ever been close enough to a donkey to smell it?" Hennie asked her.

Seti shrugged. "I don't like donkeys."

"Me either," Nef said.

I looked down at my bowl so they wouldn't see me roll my eyes.

"I think it is going to be an adventure," Hennie said cheerfully. "I am very excited."

"Tey is rather good at catching ducks," Nef said, giving me a look that suggested I should feel grateful for her kind words.

"We ate a lot of ducks on the way here." Seti sounded mournful, as if she hadn't gleefully sucked every last bone dry even while protesting she didn't like duck.

I doubted there would be many ducks in the desert. I expected to find smaller prey, such as lizards and mice. There might be foxes and lynxes and wild cats as well, but it was the lizards and mice I was counting on to supplement our supplies.

When we left later that night, we carried only a pack for each of the girls with their bed mats and the clothes they had gained since we arrived. Seti also took the little wooden men she had been playing with. It took longer than I anticipated to harness the donkeys, load all the supplies, and get them out of the barn. It had seemed straightforward when the farmer showed me what to do earlier, but the donkeys were restless and not at all inclined to stand quietly for me as they did for him.

"Do we get to ride now?" Nef asked as we left.

"Not yet," I said. "We will let them walk without burden while we can. They will have to carry us for long enough."

At the well, we filled our water containers. I had tried to surreptitiously ask around to see if anyone knew of a good route through the desert, but quickly realised I wouldn't get any useful information without saying exactly where we wanted to go. The coast was to the east of Nubet and the sun also rose in the east. So as long as we travelled towards sunrise, we would reach the coast eventually.

Once we were out of the city, I helped the girls climb up on the beasts I had assigned them. Nef forgot her pretended cynicism and grinned as she clung to her donkey. Even Seti seemed somewhat excited, although she held her nose and complained about the smell.

I helped Hennie up as well. Like the girls, she had never ridden a beast. I didn't tell them I hadn't either. They seemed to assume I had experience in such a thing and I figured that would make them more inclined to trust what I said. So I let them think I was well accustomed to riding and we set off. I clung to my donkey with my legs, even as I tried to relax my shoulders and look like I was at ease. I prayed to Aten I wouldn't be the first to fall off.

I had tied the donkeys in two columns. Behind my beast was Seti's and then half the supply animals. Hennie headed the second column, with Nef's donkey behind her and the rest of the beasts. I had also tied my donkey to Hennie's, so the two groups wouldn't become separated if we encountered a sandstorm and could no longer see each other. But with just one rope joining the two columns, I could quickly separate them with a slice of my dagger if it became necessary.

Each line of donkeys carried exactly half our supplies. If we somehow became separated, each group would have what they needed to survive. I hoped such a thing wouldn't happen, but my training had taught me to prepare for the worst.

As we headed into the desert, I waited for questions from the princesses. Seti seemed almost asleep as she leaned against her donkey's neck and it was Nef who finally asked.

"Tey, where are we going?"

"To the sea," I said, trying to sound excited. "We are going to travel all the way across Egypt until we reach the Red Sea."

"We are in the desert, though," she said.

"Yes, we are. We need to cross the desert to get to the sea."

"We are going to ride all the way across the desert?" Nef's tone was incredulous.

I glanced back to see how Seti was taking this. She sat up and frowned at her sister.

"It is an adventure," I said. "Surely I am not the only one who wants an adventure."

"I think we have had enough adventures," Nef said in a very prim tone that told me she hadn't yet forgotten she was a princess. "Where will we sleep at night?"

"Wherever we are," I said. "You remember what it was like when we sailed down the Great River to get to Nubet? We camped wherever we found a suitable spot. That is what we will do again, only we will camp in the desert."

"It is very hot in the desert," she said.

"Much hotter than on the river," Seti added.

At least we were far enough from the town that it was unlikely anyone would hear if one of them — Seti most likely — had a tantrum.

"It will be hot during the day, but the nights will be cold," I said. "I think you will be surprised to discover just how cold. We will travel at night as much as possible and rest during the day."

"Won't that be exciting?" Hennie's enthusiasm was likely for the girls' benefit and not a reflection of how she felt. "Riding donkeys across the desert under the moon. What an adventure."

"I prefer to sleep at night," Nef said.

"Me too," Seti said quickly. "I don't want to ride a donkey all night."

"It will be much more pleasant than riding through the heat of the day." Hennie turned around to look at them, although her eyesight was bad enough that they were probably no more than blurry shapes for her. "My dears, Tey knows what she is doing and she has a good plan. We need to trust her."

"How long will we be in the desert?" Nef sounded like she was considering Hennie's suggestion, but wasn't sure whether I was trustworthy.

"I don't know," I said.

"Grandmother said you have a plan." Her tone grew accusing. Obviously, I had proven myself to not be trustworthy. "If you have a plan, you must know how long we have to do this for."

I had hoped to avoid saying it. Seti, at least, wouldn't react well.

"A couple of weeks. Maybe a little more. It depends how fast the donkeys can go and how often we need to rest them."

"Weeks?" Seti's voice rose in a shriek.

"I don't want to be in the desert for weeks," Nef said. "That is too long."

"That is how long it will take us to reach the coast," I said.

"I don't want to go to the coast," Seti wailed. "I want to go back to Grandmother's house."

At least she wasn't asking to go back to the palace. And she didn't seem angry, only upset. It finally occurred to me that taking Seti through the desert might not have been the best decision, given her "bad thing's" affinity for sand.

"We cannot go back," I said. "The bad men are on their way there. Now they know where Grandmother lives, we are not safe there anymore."

"Will they take Nef again if they find us?" Seti asked.

Was she considering whether the risk to her sister was worth crossing the desert? I didn't like to think such a thing of her, but her tone was too calculating.

"I don't know," I said shortly. "They might take you this time. They might take both of you. Or they might just kill you both and be done with it. You have probably proved to be far more hassle than they expected, since it has been so hard to catch you. If it was me, I would kill you rather than risk trying to transport you back to Akhetaten."

"Are you taking us into the desert to kill us?" Nef asked.

I sighed. I shouldn't have let my temper get the best of me. Now it would take ages to convince them that wasn't what I meant. I was grateful when Hennie jumped in.

"No, dear," she said. "Tey is protecting us. She is taking us far away to where the bad men won't be able to find us. We will be safe there, but we have to get across the desert first."

"Is Tey protecting you as well, Grandmother?" Nef asked.

"She certainly is, dear. Now the bad men know I was looking after you all, they will be searching for me as well. That is why I have to come with you. We need to trust that Tey knows what she is doing. We will travel a bit longer before we stop for a break, but when we do, we will be able to have a fire. Tey told me you learnt how to build a fire on the way here. Is that right? Do you think you could show me?"

"I know how to make a fire," Seti said.

My heart sank as I realised what I had forgotten to pack: firewood. It wouldn't matter whether I could catch lizards or mice or other small creatures along the way if we couldn't cook them. I might eat them raw if I had to, but there was no way I would convince the girls to do so. How could I have forgotten such a basic necessity as firewood?

"Maybe not tonight," I said. "We are still close enough to the town that someone might see the smoke and wonder who is out here."

And perhaps as we travelled, I would see something we could burn. If I could collect bits and pieces on the way, they would think that had been my plan all along.

"But I want to show Grandmother how to make a fire," Seti wailed. "It isn't fair."

I sighed and didn't answer. It was late and I was tired and had heard enough of Seti's complaints for one day. The moon was high and almost full, providing plenty of light to see our way. The night air was chilly, but the donkey beneath me was warm. If I didn't have to listen to Seti, it was quite pleasant out here in the desert at night.

FORTY-ONE

TEY

By the time we stopped for a break and to rest the donkeys, the girls were too tired to argue about wanting to build a fire. I managed to quietly tell Hennie we didn't have any firewood.

"Never mind, dear," she said. "They will forget soon enough or you will think of something. Let's just rest while we can."

It was harder than I anticipated, travelling with a group of people who were entirely unaccustomed to the harshness of the desert. It would have been a difficult journey if I was alone, but knowing the lives of three other people, plus fifteen donkeys, depended on me made me tense and irritable.

We travelled at night as much as possible. It was kinder on the donkeys who were the ones doing the hard work. During the day, we draped cloth shelters over sticks to shield us from the sun while we rested. I figured it would get easier as we adjusted to sleeping during the day and being up all night. Or at least, I hoped it would.

At least once a day, Seti would burst into tears at the lack of something we didn't have. Even Nef became demanding. Hennie tried to keep peace between us all as best she could, but I sensed her patience growing thin.

"How *much* longer is this going to take?" Seti called.

It was midmorning and we lay beneath our shelters. They were barely big enough to sit up in, but at least they provided some shade. From the shelter Hennie and I shared, I could hear Seti tossing on her linen sheet in the girls' shelter.

"Tey, how much longer?" she called again when I didn't answer.

"How long do you think? I told you it would take at least a couple of weeks. We have been travelling for three days. How many more days will it take us to get to the coast?"

"I don't know," she said.

I gritted my teeth at the whine in her voice.

"Then figure it out," I snapped. "You must have had enough schooling to figure a sum like that."

"I don't want to. I want you to tell me."

I let out a huff of exasperation.

"I cannot take much more of her," I whispered to Hennie. "She is driving me out of my mind."

"It is the travel," she said. "It is hard on all of us. I suppose as princesses they are not used to being uncomfortable."

"They need to stop thinking of themselves as princesses. It does them no good."

"I don't know how they would do such a thing, dear. That was all they knew until the day you took them away. It must be a tough thing to adjust to. It is not so hard for the likes of you and me. We are not used to lazing on soft couches all day and having servants to do our bidding. Even so, I admit I am finding the travel more tiring than I expected."

"Are you sorry you came with us?"

She took her time answering and I thought she was trying to find an inoffensive way to agree with me. But when she spoke, I realised she must have been sorting through her thoughts.

"Not sorry, no," she said. "But perhaps I didn't think it through enough. I didn't consider the toll that travelling like this would have on an old woman."

How old was she? She had said little of her son and I didn't know how old she was when she gave birth to him, but I guessed she was in at least her mid-forties now, if not more. She was indeed an old woman, although she was still quite spry, even if her knees pained her. She couldn't see very well and her fingers sometimes looked swollen, but she was in quite good condition for a woman her age. I hadn't even considered whether our travels would be too hard on her.

"It might have been better for you to stay home," I said. "But although it is selfish of me, I am pleased you didn't. If it was just the three of us, I think I would have murdered them both by now. Or Seti at least."

Hennie chuckled.

"Oh, my dear, I don't think you see how alike the two of you are," she said.

"Me and Seti? I am nothing like her."

"Do you really think so?"

"Of course not. She is a spoiled princess and I am a commoner. Her father was Pharaoh. Mine is a foot soldier. We are nothing alike."

"You are both stubborn and strong-willed. I expect you were a handful at her age."

"At her age I was..." I paused to think. "I was pestering my father to teach me more. I probably near drove him out of his mind. He had already taught me to defend myself, but he refused to teach me anything else."

"I don't doubt you were unwilling to accept his refusals. You may have gone about it differently from Seti, though. I cannot see you having tantrums, but I am sure your father heard very often about what you wanted."

"I was determined that he would teach me. When he wouldn't, I picked a fight with the meanest boy I knew. He left me rather bruised and bloodied. When I went home like that, my father finally decided he should give me more training."

Hennie laughed.

"See, you and Seti are not so different," she said. "You have different approaches, but you are both determined to get your own way."

Outside our shelter, a donkey snorted. I listened, one hand already reaching for a dagger. Had someone found us?

"Tey?" Nef's voice was tearful.

My heart stuttered as I imagined what had happened out there while I lazed in the shade. Someone had found us and they had Nef, probably with a blade to her throat. I dived out of the shelter, my dagger ready.

Nef sat alone in the girls' shelter, her face streaked with tears.

"What happened?" I spun around, searching. "Where is he?"

"Seti is gone," she said with a sob.

"Where? Who took her?"

"She wanted to go home. She made me promise not to tell you, but I got scared." Nef sniffled. "She will hate me when she finds out I broke my promise."

Hennie leaned down to look Nef in the eyes. She rested one hand against Nef's cheek.

"Nef, dear, tell us what happened," she said. "Why did Seti leave and where has she gone?"

"She doesn't like being out here," Nef said. "She has gone home."

"Where is home, dear? The palace?"

Nef wiped her nose with the back of her hand and shook her head.

"Your house."

Seti's donkey was gone and the ropes that had secured it to the others were cut. I sliced through the rope securing my beast and mounted him.

"Stay here," I called. "I will find her. Nef, which way did she go?"

Nef pointed. I could just make out the donkey's tracks in the sand, although they were disappearing fast, helped along by a light wind.

"Aten damn that child," I muttered.

"What do you need me to do?" Hennie asked.

"Make sure Nef doesn't follow and that we don't lose any of the donkeys. Check whether she thought to cut the other ropes. She may have figured she could stop us from following her if we had to chase after the donkeys."

I set off in pursuit of Seti.

FORTY-TWO
SETI

I was angry when Tey wouldn't tell me how much longer we had to stay in the desert. I was too little to have to figure things out for myself. The bad thing was turning around in my belly. It wanted to come out, just like it always did when I got angry. I didn't want the bad thing to come out. Not after what happened last time with the boat. I squeezed my eyes shut and told myself I wasn't angry anymore.

Eventually, the bad thing stopped turning around. It was only after that I remembered how Tey had told me to breathe when I needed to keep the bad thing inside.

My stomach was grumbling and it had been hours since we broke our fast. I went to the donkeys and rummaged through a basket of supplies, looking for something to eat. My fingers found a dagger. It must have been one of Tey's spares because Hennie didn't have daggers, and neither did Nef. I slid it from its sheath and the blade was smooth and sharp. It was only then I made a plan to escape.

I had thought about going back to Grandmother's house before, but the donkeys were all tied together. I had looked at the knots a couple of times and even had a poke at one to see if I could undo it, but Tey had tied them and they were tight. The only way I would get my donkey away from the others was if I had a dagger. And now I did. I went back to our shelter.

"Nef," I whispered.

"Go away," she murmured. "I am sleeping."

"Nef, I need to talk to you."

"Not now."

She rolled over, putting her back to me. I kicked some sand over her feet.

"Seti!" She sat up and brushed the sand off. "I want to sleep."

"But I need to tell you something."

"Fine." She sighed, just like Tey did when she thought I was being annoying. It was a hurtful thing for Nef to do, but I decided to forgive her. "What is it?"

"I am going back to Grandmother's house."

She made her eyes very wide and shook her head.

"We are going to the coast," she said. "Tey says we cannot go back to Grandmother's."

"Well, I am going and Tey will have to catch me if she wants to stop me."

"You know she probably can. Besides, Grandmother isn't even there."

"I know that." I rolled my eyes the way Tey did sometimes when she thought we weren't looking. "But if I go home, Tey will have to bring you and Grandmother back to find me. And then we can all stay there."

It was a good plan. It made me feel happy.

"But what about the bad men?" Nef asked.

I shrugged. I hadn't thought about them, but Tey had kept us safe from the bad men so far. Even when they stole Nef, she went and found her again. I tried not to think about how Nef almost went to the West, but she came back because I told her all my memories. Even if she didn't remember, I knew that must have been what made her better.

"They already got me once, Seti," Nef said. "They will be angry

Tey found me. They will probably just kill me straight away if they find me again."

"Then you can stay here."

I felt bad that Nef couldn't come back to Grandmother's house with me, but I didn't want to be in the desert any more. I didn't like riding a smelly donkey and I hated not being able to sleep at night. I didn't like the way I always had sand all over me. It made my skin itch. And it was hot out here. Except at night, when it was freezing cold. Even with a blanket around my shoulders and a warm donkey beneath me, I was still cold all night.

"I am going to tell Tey," Nef said. She even started to get up. "She won't let you go."

"No." I grabbed her hand to stop her. "Nef, you cannot tell her. Please."

Nef shook her head and gave me a mean look. She pulled her hand out of mine, but I grabbed it again.

"Don't you love me anymore?" I made my voice as sad as I could.

"Of course I do," she said. "We are sisters."

"If you tell Tey I am leaving, I will know you don't love me. You probably want the bad men to find me so they will kill me."

"Don't say things like that," Nef said crossly. "You know it is not true."

"If you tell Tey, it is."

We glared at each other until Nef gave in.

"Fine," she said. "I won't tell her you are leaving. But what do I do when she realises you are gone and asks me where you went?"

"Just say you don't know," I said, happy now I knew Nef loved me again. "You can say I left while you were sleeping."

She frowned at me.

"Seti, this is a bad idea."

I leaned over to kiss her cheek.

"Bye, Nef."

I hurried my donkey in the direction Nef had indicated. Already the sand was settling over the tracks and I had nothing to guide me other than the general direction. If Seti planned to go to Hennie's home, she was going the wrong way. She needed to go west, but instead she headed north. Further into the vast expanse of desert.

I urged my donkey on. I had already realised my mistake in leaving without even a jug of beer or some water for the beast. We would not last long out here without something to drink. But presumably Seti had taken no supplies either. She would survive for an even shorter time than I would.

For more than an hour, I went north. Seti might easily become disorientated and deviate from her path, so I watched all around me for any sign of her. But there was nothing. No tracks. No excrement from her donkey. Nothing. I wondered whether Nef had sent me in the wrong direction. Had she felt bad enough to tell me Seti was gone, but not bad enough to tell the truth about where?

The wind blew harder, and I unwrapped my headscarf to tie it over my nose and mouth. Since I left Hennie and Nef, the sky had become an ominous shade of orange. Sand flew past my face and I couldn't see much further than the length of a couple of men. I had only been in a sandstorm twice before, but I knew what was coming.

"Seti!" I called, even though I knew it was futile.

Would she know what to do in a sandstorm? Somehow, I doubted the princess ever had to cope with such a thing on her own. Guards or servants would have rushed her to shelter if a sandstorm hit Akhetaten. But perhaps this storm wasn't natural. It might be Seti's own creation.

The sand was closing in around me and I could see no further than the tip of my donkey's nose. There was no point continuing. I didn't even know what direction we travelled in anymore. I dismounted and urged the beast to lie down. Then I crouched beside him with my face against his flank, drew my headscarf up over my head, and waited.

The storm lasted for hours. The wind swirled furiously, whipping sand across my arms and neck. I didn't dare try to check whether I was bleeding. My mouth grew dry and sticky. It didn't matter that I had nothing to drink when I couldn't risk opening my mouth without taking in a mouthful of sand. The wind buffeted me from side to side and I thought it would lift me right off the ground. I clung to the donkey and prayed to Aten the storm would subside soon.

Had Seti had the sense to cover her face and get down from her donkey? Maybe her ability gave her some way of protecting herself. Perhaps she could hold the wind at bay around her. Or perhaps she had created this storm herself to keep me from finding her. She might not even know she had done it. I hoped a storm of this magnitude was beyond her, but I didn't know how strong her "bad thing" was.

By the time the storm eased, I was buried in sand up to my shoulders. My legs cramped and my back was stiff as I struggled to get to my feet. I swept the sand off the donkey and urged the beast up. He shook sand from his ears and blew it from his nose with a great snort. Like me, scrapes and scratches covered his body, but neither of us had sustained anything more than minor wounds.

The landscape looked different now, the shapes of the dunes changed. The donkey was probably as exhausted as I was, so I walked beside him. We made our way up a nearby dune and I prayed with every step I would see Seti. But when we reached the top, my heart sank. All around us, as far as I could see, was sand. No sign of Seti or her donkey. No sign of our campsite.

FORTY-FOUR

TEY

I felt helpless as I tried to figure out what to do. Did I continue on after Seti or try to find my way back to our camp? I might not find her before we both perished from dehydration. Perhaps it would be better to return to Hennie and Nef, get some supplies, and go after Seti again? But I didn't know how much of a head start she had on me and going back to our camp might take a half a day or more, especially if I had veered off course. Those hours could be the difference between Seti dying of thirst and me finding her in time.

I stood at the top of that dune for far too long, unable to decide. Come on, Tey. Make a decision. Any decision is better than standing here doing nothing.

I decided to go back for supplies. I would be of no help to Seti if I found her, but couldn't get her back to camp before we both perished. And if I died, what would happen to Nef and Hennie? To look after all of them, I needed to look after myself first.

The sky was still murky, and I wasn't sure where the sun was, but I picked the direction I thought was east, climbed up on the donkey, and set off. I kept a careful watch on either side of me, in case my sense of direction was off, but saw no sign of our camp.

At length I stopped. The donkey had walked for at least an hour and I still wasn't sure we were even going the right way. Perhaps I should wait until I could see the sky more clearly and get a better sense of my direction. Then again, I might be so far off course that even if I went due east, I wouldn't spot the camp.

Papa would be ashamed if he could see me now. One sandstorm and I was disorientated. I was lost in the desert with no supplies, one of my charges was missing, and I was so dehydrated that it was becoming difficult to think straight.

Think, Tey. You know there is a solution. You just have to focus long enough to find it.

But my thoughts slid all over the place and all I wanted to do was lie down in the sand and go to sleep. My heart beat far too fast, I was breathing too hard, and my head swam.

I found myself face down in the sand. It stuck to my cheeks, hot and prickly. The beast plodded on, seeming to not notice his sudden lack of rider.

"Wait," I whispered, unable to speak any louder. "Come back."

But the donkey walked away.

It was too much effort to get up, so I lay there. It was only once the donkey was gone that I realised I could have slit his throat and drunk his blood. That would have sustained me long enough to come up with another plan. But it was too late. With nothing else to do, I closed my eyes and slept.

I woke when somebody shook my shoulder. I tried to open my eyes, but they seemed glued shut. A shadow passed over me, a brief respite from the sun beating down. Somebody rolled me over and peeled back one of my eyelids.

A man stared down at me. His mouth moved, but I heard nothing other than a stream of gibberish. I closed my eyes. I couldn't speak to him, so what reason did I have to stay awake? And I was so, so sleepy.

Then somebody lifted me out of the sand and draped me over a donkey, face down across its body. Somebody walked beside the donkey with a hand on my back so I didn't fall off.

The donkey's movement jolted me and my head spun. Stars

sparkled around the edges of my vision and I closed my eyes. I
didn't care where they were taking me.

FORTY-FIVE
TEY

I slowly swam back into consciousness. I had been in a deep
sleep and it was difficult to drag myself out of it. When I
opened my eyes, I found I lay on a blanket beneath a cloth shelter.
A lamp hanging from one of the shelter's supports gave off a dim
light. I smelled fire and roasting meat. Nearby, people were talking,
but I could make out nothing of what they said. A baby cried and
was quickly shushed.

It took a great effort to sit up. My limbs wobbled and my head
swam. My mouth was dry and my heart felt like it beat too fast. On
a blanket beside me lay Seti. She seemed to be asleep.

I reached for her, but the distance was too far, or maybe I was
too weak. Beside me was a mug. I managed to raise it to my lips
and drink, although not without dripping it down my front. It was
milk, perhaps from a donkey or maybe even a goat, creamy and
delicious.

A woman entered the tent and took the mug from me.

"No, I need more."

Did I speak the words or did I only think them? I couldn't be
sure.

She chattered at me, shaking her head, but I didn't understand
anything she said. She set the mug down out of my reach.

"Please," I whispered.

The woman crouched to inspect Seti, placing her hand on the girl's forehead.

"Is she well?" I asked.

The woman smiled and said something. I finally realised she was speaking in a foreign language. Although I couldn't understand her, her apparent lack of concern about Seti's condition reassured me. She spooned a little of something from a nearby bowl into the girl's mouth, then gestured for me to lie down.

Since my legs didn't seem to be strong enough to get up, I did. She chattered at me for another few moments, then left. With nothing else to do, I slept again.

When I next woke, it was day and Seti was sitting up, eating from a bowl. She noticed me stir and gave me a pitiful look.

"Seti," I said.

"I am sorry, Tey." Her face crumpled. "I should not have left."

"No, you should not have. Where are we?"

She shrugged.

"There is a woman, but I cannot understand her."

Nestled into the sand beside me was a mug. I vaguely remembered drinking from it during the night and a woman taking it away from me. At the time I didn't understand, but now my head was clearer, I realised she had been trying to stop me from making myself sick by drinking too much. I managed to sit up and sip the milk, even though I wanted to gulp it all down.

A woman appeared in the shelter's doorway. I wasn't sure whether she was the same one who had come in during the night. She smiled when she saw me sitting up, then disappeared again. She returned a few moments later and offered me a bowl and a spoon.

It was a thick gruel of some sort, warm and tasty. Strength returned to me as I ate, and by the time I emptied the bowl, I felt like I could stand. I got to my feet slowly. My head swam more than I expected and I almost toppled over.

"Wait here," I said to Seti. "I am going to see where we are."

Before I could go any further, Hennie appeared in the doorway.

"I thought she might be saying you were awake," she said with a broad smile. "How do you feel? How is Seti? They wouldn't let us in until you were both awake."

Nef pushed past her and rushed to Seti's side. They wrapped their arms around each other and cried.

"Well enough," I said. "Where are we?"

"A Sand Wanderers camp. There are two men who speak passable Egyptian. They told us one of their scout groups spotted a donkey without a rider, so they searched the area and found you lying in the sand. By the time they brought you back to their camp, another group of scouts had found Seti. They figured a woman and a girl would not be travelling alone in the desert and thought the sandstorm might have separated you from your party. They sent out other scouts who found Nef and I. They brought us all here and we have been waiting for you both to wake up."

"The sandstorm?"

Just listening to her exhausted me and I found I didn't have the strength to say any more.

"It was terrible," Hennie said. "The shelter fell on top of us, but at least we had something over us. And all the donkeys were still there when it stopped, so we didn't lose any supplies."

"I would have died if they hadn't found me."

"They said you were half dead. Seti was still on her donkey, although the poor beast could go no further. The scout said they didn't think she even realised the donkey wasn't moving."

"Thank Aten they found us."

"Come outside. Let's give the girls a little privacy."

Hennie took my arm to steady me as we walked.

"Hennie, do you think Seti did it? Did she make the sandstorm?"

Hennie gave a heavy sigh.

"I don't know, Tey, and that is the truth. I am not sure I even want to ask her. It might just give her ideas she didn't already have."

The camp seemed to consist of a dozen shelters grouped in a tight circle. Outside the circle, men, women and children were going about their day. Somebody dried strips of meat over a low fire. Laundry aired over a wooden frame. A couple of children chased each other and a pair of old men sat side by side on a blanket, watching everything that happened. Further away, a man stood guard. He looked alert as he studied the surrounding landscape.

I turned towards the sound of splashing water and discovered the camp was next to an oasis. Patches of knee high scrubby bushes, a few dom palm trees, and a shallow lake which was a brilliant shade of blue. The splashing came from the water a woman was tipping over herself as she bathed.

"Oh." I had heard of oases but had never seen one before. I hadn't expected it to be so beautiful.

"This is a temporary camp of the Sand Wanderers," Hennie said. "They told me they travel from oasis to oasis. When food becomes scarce in one location, they move to another."

"We were very fortunate they happened to be here."

"I am grateful they found you. Both of you. I shudder to think what Nef and I would have done otherwise. How long we might have waited thinking you would return when you could."

"At least you had plenty of supplies for just the two of you," I said. "You could have rationed them and survived for weeks."

"But if you hadn't returned and the Sand Wanderers hadn't found you, weeks wouldn't have been long enough. Nobody would have happened on us. Eventually we would have had to try to make our own way to the coast, or back to Nubet, or we would have perished waiting."

"But that didn't happen," I said. "We are safe now. The Sand Wanderers are good people. I remember my father talking about them. I am sure they will let us stay for a couple of days while Seti and I recover. We will head towards the coast again as soon as we are both strong enough."

"Maybe we don't have to go to the coast," Hennie suggested. "We could stay here."

"With the Sand Wanderers?"

She shrugged and gestured around us.

"There are several families here," she said. "Children for the girls to play with. They have plenty of food, although it is rather different from what we are used to. If we show ourselves to be useful, perhaps they would take us in. Wouldn't we be safer with a tribe than trying to eke out a lonely existence in a cave?"

I had thought she agreed the coast was the best option. Hurt filled me at realising she probably hated the idea. Why hadn't she said something?

"We don't need to decide right now," I said. "Let's rest for a couple of days and see what we make of things here."

FORTY-SIX

TEY

Nef and Seti seemed to settle in without fuss. They made friends with a pair of girls around the same age and the fact they spoke no common language didn't seem to bother any of them. Hennie helped the women with their chores, which seemed to involve hours of food preparation every day, and took a turn in minding the youngest children. One of the women drew an elaborate pattern over Hennie's hands and wrists, just like the tribe's women wore, and Hennie beamed with delight when she showed me.

I made myself useful where I could by taking a share of the guard duties, and soon the scouts invited me to go out with them. I thought I knew a lot about surviving in the desert, but they taught me much more. One of the scouts spoke Egyptian and as we travelled, he began teaching me the language of the Sand Wanderers. We had been here for a week, although it felt like much longer.

The Sand Wanderers provided us with a hide shelter of our own, although the girls often spent the night with their friends. I tried not to worry when they were out of my sight. The tribe was meticulous in ensuring there were always at least two men on watch duty and I doubted anyone could sneak into their camp during the night to steal the girls away.

"I think we should move on," I said to Hennie as we prepared for bed one evening. "We have been here more than two weeks and it isn't fair to let the girls settle in so much. Better we leave as soon as possible. Seti and I are both plenty strong enough."

"Have you thought about my suggestion?" she asked.

"That we stay here? Do you still feel the same?"

"I like it here. There is a sense of community I have never experienced before. The girls have friends and you seem to have found your place within the tribe."

"I am merely trying to be helpful. To repay their kindness."

"We were looking for a safe place for the girls. Do you think there is anywhere safer? It will only be a few more weeks before the tribe moves to the next oasis. What better place to hide the girls than amid a group of people who do not live in one location?"

"Their scouts are very good," I conceded. "And the men all seem to have at least some ability to fight. I have seen them training."

"So we are safe. I feel like we have found a home here, Tey. That is not something I expected with your plan to live in a cave."

"I could have built us a house." I felt a little disgruntled at her criticism. "It didn't have to be a cave."

"I know, but we would have been on our own. If one of the girls was sick or injured, we would have no resources other than our own knowledge and what herbs we could find nearby. Here, we have people. Community. Knowledge. One of the old women knows about all the desert plants and their medical uses. She has been talking to me about them, but I don't yet understand their language enough to follow most of it. I would love the chance to learn more."

"What about schooling for the girls?"

"They had private tutors, from what they have told me. They have probably already had more schooling than most girls receive. Besides, what need have they for reading or sums? There is much they can learn here, more practical things."

"I don't know. I need to think about it. We don't even know

whether they would welcome us to stay. Perhaps they are just giving us time to recover and expect us to leave soon."

"We should ask. See if they are open to us staying. I think we could contribute much here, Tey. It is not like we would be sitting on our behinds all day and taking whatever they offer. I feel like *I* could contribute."

"I will think about it, but that is all I am promising."

Hennie's words were on my mind over the next couple of days. I paid careful attention to how the Sand Wanderers interacted with us, trying to sense any sign of frustration or impatience with our continued presence. But they seemed content to have us in their midst.

I saw little of the girls, so absorbed were they with their new friends. They were receiving some kind of lessons, although it was nothing I recognised as the schooling an Egyptian child would learn, and began dressing in the way of the tribe's girls, with long dark-coloured gowns and a scarf tied over their hair. Where they procured the clothes from, I didn't know. They ran around barefooted and Seti never once complained her feet hurt. They asked Hennie to cut off their sidelocks and were letting their hair grow, so they looked more like the other children. Even Nef began to smile. I had to admit, they were thriving here.

As we patrolled one morning, I approached one of the scouts who spoke Egyptian.

"Do you think we would be welcome if we wanted to stay?" I asked. "I am not sure of the protocols. Would we ask Old Man for permission?"

Old Man was, as best I understood, the tribe's chief. He seemed to make the decisions, at any rate, and he received the choicest cuts when they slaughtered a donkey.

"Oh." He gave me a confused look. "Everyone assumed you intended to stay when you and Hennie began helping with the chores. All members of the tribe contribute in whatever capacity they are able, but we would never allow guests to work."

"Does that mean we are already part of the tribe?"

He shrugged at me, clearly confused.

"Of course."

I told Hennie about my conversation that evening.

"They are happy for us to stay?" she asked.

"They seem to think we have already decided."

"And have you?"

"Not yet. I feel like if we were to stay, it would have to be temporary. An interim home. I am not sure such a lifestyle would be good for the girls."

"I have never seen them smile so much as they have since we arrived," Hennie said. "They love it here."

"That is what makes this decision so difficult. The longer we stay, the more settled they will become. It is inevitable someone will find us, sooner or later. And what then? We tear the girls away from everything they know yet again? Force them to leave their friends behind? Their home?"

"They have survived it before and they will do so again if they must. But, Tey dear, you are looking for trouble. There is no reason to think anyone will find us out here. And if they do, we will deal with it, and at least we will have help. I don't think there is a safer place for the girls in all of Egypt."

I didn't tell her I had considered not staying in Egypt. One reason I suggested going to the coast was so we could more easily get out of the country if we needed to flee. We could have secured passage on a ship and sailed away. Rome, Indou, Babylonia were all places I had considered. Syria, Thrace or Mycenae even. If Egypt was no longer safe, there were plenty of places we could go.

Papa had taught both Intef and me much about geography, certainly far more than either of us learnt at school. He always said a soldier would never regret understanding the world around him. I fiddled with my mother's ring as I thought about Papa. I missed him, even though I didn't let myself think about him often. It hurt too much to know I would never see him again.

"Let me think about it a little longer," I said.

"Fine, but don't take too long. If you are determined to leave, we should do it soon. The girls get more settled every day."

I decided to ask Nef and Seti what they wanted. It wasn't fair for me to make this decision for everyone without asking. Hennie had made her position clear — she wanted to stay and I assumed the girls did, too — but I should at least ask. Perhaps they were only making the best of the situation and expected to move on soon.

I waited for a chance to speak with them, but I couldn't catch them when the other children weren't around. A couple of days passed before I found Nef on her own.

"I need to talk to you and Seti," I said. "Where is she?"

She shrugged, too intent on something she was making with a handful of dom palm nuts and a length of cord.

"I haven't seen her for a while," she said.

My heart raced and I paused to make sure my voice was steady before I replied. I didn't want to alarm Nef over something that was probably nothing.

"Where did you see her last?" I asked.

She nodded towards the west.

"She went that way," she said.

"By herself?"

"I think so."

"Stay here. Don't wander off. I will be back as soon as I find her."

I headed in the direction she indicated. Seti was nowhere to be seen. I started to run, but I didn't call out to her. If someone had found her, I didn't want to alert them to my presence.

FORTY-SEVEN
SETI

Everyone was busy doing things and, for once, it seemed like nobody was watching me. Not even Tey. Maybe that meant I could do some practising with the bad thing. If I could make it do what I wanted it to, maybe I wouldn't be so scared of it. It wouldn't listen to me when the sandstorm hit. I tried to convince it to come out and protect me, but it wouldn't, and that made me more determined than ever to figure it out. Maybe I could even use it to protect Nef and me the next time the bad men came.

I wandered away from the camp, trying to pretend I wasn't going anywhere in particular. There was a sand dune not far away and nobody could spy on me if I went behind it. I looked back over my shoulder a few times, but nobody followed.

As I reached the dune, I turned back towards the camp and stretched out my arms as if I was just enjoying the sun falling on my skin. Was Aten watching me? Did he know I was about to let go of the bad thing? Would he tell my father? After all, Father was supposed to be a star up in the sky now. I supposed that meant he might talk to Aten sometimes.

Since nobody yelled at me to come back to camp, I hurried around the side of the dune. I could breathe better once I was out of sight. I found a nice spot to stop and let my toes sink down into the sand. My feet had gotten used to walking on hot sand and I liked its warmth against my soles.

"You can come out now, bad thing," I said.

I waited, but nothing happened.

"Come on. There is nobody to see you here."

But if the bad thing heard me, it didn't come.

It had always just come out before, even when I didn't want it to. Always except for during the sandstorm.

I tried to remember the times I felt the bad thing. When I saw Tey carrying Nef off the boat, I got really scared and then really mad. And when she told me to go into the house when I just wanted to play with Grandmother's little wooden men, I got mad then too. So maybe the bad thing only listened to me if I was angry.

I thought about all the things that made me mad. I didn't like it when Tey said I had to have a bath before I went to bed, but it didn't make me mad. It made me mad, though, when she kept saying we couldn't go home. I was a princess. I wasn't supposed to sleep in the sand. I was supposed to have soft beds and servants to bring me bath water and hot dinners any time I wanted them.

The bad thing fluttered inside me. At first, it felt like I might have eaten something my tummy didn't like. Then it felt like I was going to vomit. But the bad thing didn't come out of me and I needed it to. I thought some more about hot dinners and palaces and soft beds, and I started getting really mad about all the things Tey didn't let me have.

The bad thing shot straight up my throat and flew out of me. Sand swirled around my feet. Not very high, but enough that I knew the bad thing was there.

"Seti!" came Tey's voice.

The sand dropped and the bad thing disappeared back down inside me as Tey ran over.

"What are you doing?" She put her hands on her hips and frowned at me.

I shrugged and tried not to look at her.

"Practising," I said.

"Seti, you promised you wouldn't do that."

"I need to learn how to make the bad thing do what I want it to."

"No, you don't. You need to forget you can do that. It isn't safe. Have you already forgotten what happened last time?"

"But that is why I need to learn. So I can figure out how to make it listen to me. So when the bad men come after us again, I can use it on them."

"No, Seti, I forbid it. You are not to do that again. You could hurt someone. You could hurt yourself. Promise me you will never do this again."

"You said you would find someone to teach me, but you didn't."

"I will try to find someone," she said. "When I can. Now promise me."

I stared down at the sand and shook my head.

"Seti."

Tey's voice sounded like a warning. She had seemed scared before, but now she was mad at me. Maybe she had a bad thing inside her, too.

"I need to know how," I said. "What if you aren't around when the bad men come?"

"You don't need to worry about that as long as you don't wander off on your own."

"If I knew how to make it work, I could have stopped them when they took Nef."

"Seti." Tey crouched in front of me and made me look at her. "I know this has been difficult, for you and for Nef. My job is to protect you both, but I cannot do that if you keep wandering off by yourself and doing things I have told you not to. Please, I need you to listen to me and do what I say. Will you promise me you will not experiment with your ability any more?"

I nodded, although I didn't say anything. Hopefully, she wouldn't realise I hadn't actually promised. I would have to wait for another time to practice with the bad thing.

"Come on, then." Tey held out her hand to me. "I need to talk to you and Nef. Let's go back to the camp."

FORTY-EIGHT
TEY

We went back to Nef, then went to find Hennie who was waiting in the shelter she and I shared. The girls looked at me expectantly and I realised I didn't know what to say. I should have spent some time preparing my words before I tried to talk to them.

"Do you like it here?" I asked.

They glanced at each other and each seemed to wait for the other to speak first.

"Nef?" I prodded.

She shrugged. "It is not as good as the palace."

How long would it be before their first reaction was not that of a princess? Perhaps that would never change. Maybe they were too steeped in that world to leave it behind.

"What about you, Seti?" I asked.

She exhaled, although I couldn't tell whether it was supposed to be a huff or a sigh.

"I suppose it is not that bad," she said. "I would rather live in a palace, though."

"You promised we would have a house," Nef reminded me. "You said we would have beds and baths, even if we had to share a bedchamber with you."

"I did."

I glanced at Hennie to see what she thought of their responses. She gave me a little shrug, as if to say it was my decision. Or perhaps that she didn't know what to do.

"Maybe it is time for us to move on," I said. "Go to the coast like we planned. You will like it there. You can swim in the sea and play in the sand. We will eat fresh fish every day."

"I don't want to," Seti said. She crossed her arms over her chest.

"Stay calm, Seti. We are just talking. Besides, from what you just said, I didn't think you wanted to stay."

"Well, I do," she said. "I would rather go back to the palace, but if we cannot do that because of the bad men, then I want to stay here."

"Me too," Nef said.

"But don't you want a house and beds and baths?"

They looked at each other for a few moments.

"The sand is kind of soft for a bed," Nef said. "Once you put a blanket over the top and get the sand just right, it is not uncomfortable."

"I like bathing in the oasis," Seti said. "And I don't want to leave my friends."

"We haven't had friends before," Nef said. "I don't want to go."

Would they tire of a nomadic lifestyle? Perhaps the first time the tribe moved on, they might decide that travelling from oasis to oasis was not what they wanted.

"We must never forget the bad men are still looking for you," I said. "There might come a day when I tell you we have to leave. If that happens, I mean it, all right? If I say we need to leave, you grab your things and get ready to go immediately. It will mean the bad men are close by and we have to run."

"That sounds fair," Nef said.

"All right," Seti added.

I looked at Hennie.

"What about you, Hennie? You should have a say in this too. Do you agree we should stay?"

Hennie looked at each of the girls, but at length, she nodded.

"I think we should stay," she said. "For now, at least."

"I suppose that is it then," I said. "We will stay with the Sand Wanderers for now. Just until the bad men get too close."

"Can we go play now?" Seti asked, giving me a bright smile as she jumped to her feet.

"Go on," I said. "You both look rather grubby. Make sure you take a bath before you go to bed tonight."

"Come on, Nef," Seti said.

Nef got up a little more slowly and paused to look at me.

"Something you want to say?" I asked.

"Thank you for keeping us safe," she said.

She leaned down to give me a quick kiss on the cheek, then ran off with Seti.

The journey continues in Book 2: *Catalyst*

They thought they had found a safe place to call home. They were wrong.

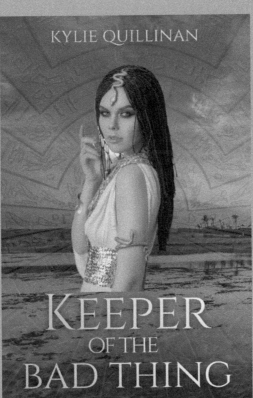

KYLIE QUILLINAN

KEEPER
OF THE
BAD THING

A SHORT STORY IN THE WORLD OF
THE AMARNA AGE

ALSO BY KYLIE QUILLINAN

The Amarna Princesses Series

Book One: *Outcast*

Book Two: *Catalyst*

Book Three: *Warrior*

The Amarna Age Series

Book One: *Queen of Egypt*

Book Two: *Son of the Hittites*

Book Three: *Eye of Horus*

Book Four: *Gates of Anubis*

Book Five: *Lady of the Two Lands*

Book Six: *Guardian of the Underworld*

Daughter of the Sun: An Amarna Age Novella

Palace of the Ornaments Series

Book One: *Princess of Babylon*

Book Two: *Ornament of Pharaoh*

Book Three: *Child of the Alliance*

Book Four: *A Game of Senet*

Book Five: *Secrets of Pharaoh*

Book Six: *Hawk of the West*

See kyliequillinan.com for more books, including exclusive collections, and newsletter sign up.

ABOUT THE AUTHOR

Kylie writes about women who defy society's expectations. Her novels are for readers who like fantasy with a basis in history or mythology. Her interests include Dr Who, jellyfish and cocktails. She needs to get fit before the zombies come.

Swan – the epilogue to the Tales of Silver Downs series – is available exclusively to her newsletter subscribers. Sign up at kyliequillinan.com.

Printed in the USA
CPSIA information can be obtained
at www.ICGtesting.com
LVHW042150180923
758594LV00031B/548